It was time to take his leave

Mack Bolan increased the Mustang's speed, determined not to let Guerra's men get away. Inside the large, nylon bag on the seat next to him was an arsenal of assorted weapons for making war.

Bolan raced toward the carnage ahead of him and slammed on the brakes at the last moment, swinging his vehicle around to the outside of the sedan as he reached into the bag and withdrew the MP-5. He depressed the trigger and swept the vehicle. The bodies of the gunners danced under the massive assault. Bolan then yanked an M-67 high-explosive grenade and tossed it casually into the interior, before putting the Mustang in Reverse and backing out.

The blast produced enough force to lift the car an inch or two off its wheels and settle it back to the pavement in a roaring crash.

That would teach Mario Guerra a lesson—make him realize he and his Hillbangers weren't quite as invincible as they had thought. And Guerra would learn one more thing very soon....

The Executioner was just getting started.

MACK BOLAN ®

The Executioner

#300 Warrior's Requiem
#301 Blast Radius
#302 Shadow Search
#303 Sea of Terror
#304 Soviet Specter
#305 Point Position
#306 Mercy Mission
#307 Hard Pursuit
#308 Into the Fire
#309 Flames of Fury
#310 Killing Heat
#311 Night of the Knives
#312 Death Gamble
#313 Lockdown
#314 Lethal Payload
#315 Agent of Peril
#316 Poison Justice
#317 Hour of Judgment
#318 Code of Resistance
#319 Entry Point
#320 Exit Code
#321 Suicide Highway
#322 Time Bomb
#323 Soft Target
#324 Terminal Zone
#325 Edge of Hell
#326 Blood Tide
#327 Serpent's Lair
#328 Triangle of Terror
#329 Hostile Crossing
#330 Dual Action
#331 Assault Force
#332 Slaughter House
#333 Aftershock
#334 Jungle Justice
#335 Blood Vector
#336 Homeland Terror
#337 Tropic Blast

#338 Nuclear Reaction
#339 Deadly Contact
#340 Splinter Cell
#341 Rebel Force
#342 Double Play
#343 Border War
#344 Primal Law
#345 Orange Alert
#346 Vigilante Run
#347 Dragon's Den
#348 Carnage Code
#349 Firestorm
#350 Volatile Agent
#351 Hell Night
#352 Killing Trade
#353 Black Death Reprise
#354 Ambush Force
#355 Outback Assault
#356 Defense Breach
#357 Extreme Justice
#358 Blood Toll
#359 Desperate Passage
#360 Mission to Burma
#361 Final Resort
#362 Patriot Acts
#363 Face of Terror
#364 Hostile Odds
#365 Collision Course
#366 Pele's Fire
#367 Loose Cannon
#368 Crisis Nation
#369 Dangerous Tides
#370 Dark Alliance
#371 Fire Zone
#372 Lethal Compound
#373 Code of Honor
#374 System Corruption
#375 Salvador Strike

The Don Pendleton's®
Executioner®
SALVADOR STRIKE

A GOLD EAGLE BOOK FROM
W❂RLDWIDE®

TORONTO • NEW YORK • LONDON
AMSTERDAM • PARIS • SYDNEY • HAMBURG
STOCKHOLM • ATHENS • TOKYO • MILAN
MADRID • WARSAW • BUDAPEST • AUCKLAND

Recycling programs
for this product may
not exist in your area.

First edition February 2010

ISBN-13: 978-0-373-64375-2

Special thanks and acknowledgment to Jon Guenther for his contribution to this work.

SALVADOR STRIKE

Printed in U.S.A.

The future of civilization depends on our overcoming the meaninglessness and hopelessness characterized by the thoughts of men today.

—Albert Schweitzer
1875–1965

There are men whose abilities to contribute positive energies on the world are blinded by their greed and lust for power. It is those men who subject the innocent to meaningless and hopeless lives. I shall resist them in every waking moment.

—Mack Bolan

THE
MACK BOLAN
LEGEND

Nothing less than a war could have fashioned the destiny of the man called Mack Bolan. Bolan earned the Executioner title in the jungle hell of Vietnam.

But this soldier also wore another name—Sergeant Mercy. He was so tagged because of the compassion he showed to wounded comrades-in-arms and Vietnamese civilians.

Mack Bolan's second tour of duty ended prematurely when he was given emergency leave to return home and bury his family, victims of the Mob. Then he declared a one-man war against the Mafia.

He confronted the Families head-on from coast to coast, and soon a hope of victory began to appear. But Bolan had broken society's every rule. That same society started gunning for this elusive warrior—to no avail.

So Bolan was offered amnesty to work within the system against terrorism. This time, as an employee of Uncle Sam, Bolan became Colonel John Phoenix. With a command center at Stony Man Farm in Virginia, he and his new allies—Able Team and Phoenix Force—waged relentless war on a new adversary: the KGB.

But when his one true love, April Rose, died at the hands of the Soviet terror machine, Bolan severed all ties with Establishment authority.

Now, after a lengthy lone-wolf struggle and much soul-searching, the Executioner has agreed to enter an "arm's-length" alliance with his government once more, reserving the right to pursue personal missions in his Everlasting War.

Prologue

Herndon, Virginia

Gary Marciano, federal prosecutor for the Attorney General of the United States, studied the early-morning edition of the newspaper with immense satisfaction.

Over his bowl of sliced bananas on oatmeal topped with milk and honey, Marciano reread the bold, front page headline: National Gang Members Charged with RICO Violations. At last! Several key members of MS-13 were in custody and based on the pages of testimony by his key witness—testimony submitted and leading to indictments by a federal grand jury last week—these domestic terror mongers wouldn't be spreading any more violence or bloodshed for a long time, if ever again. The suburban neighborhoods of Virginia, Florida and California would be safer with those bastards out of the picture.

Marciano thought of Ysidro Perez, the one brave soul who decided to get his life together and make a stand. With no thought for his own safety, Perez voluntarily stepped out on his homeboys in Virginia—a cell dubbed the Hillbangers by local law enforcement—to report on their activities and betray the sacred trust extended to him. Perez's testimony had eventually led to not only the arrest of his leader, Mario Guerra, but six other high-ranking members from various cells throughout the United States.

And that's only the beginning, Marciano thought.

The prosecutor dropped the paper on the table and turned to finishing his breakfast. The Bulova watch on his wrist, a Christmas present from his wife, told him he had only a few minutes before he had to leave for his office. Rush-hour traffic had grown worse over the past couple of years, as well as the construction of new homes in what had once been a quiet development, which ultimately tacked more than twenty minutes onto what had once been a ten-minute commute. It took him nearly a half hour to drive barely ten miles.

Sad, that's what it was.

Marciano finished about half of his breakfast and then rose, scraped the remainder into the garbage can and rinsed out the bowl. He left it in the sink, confident Caroline would take care of it like she always did. Faithful and diligent, his adoring wife had stayed home with their three kids during their early years, but when the youngest finally reached seventh grade, she took a job selling real estate in a booming market. Marciano knew she was a shoo-in for such a position; it suited Caroline's impeccable tastes and uncanny ability to match the right perspective buyer with the right place.

They didn't really need the money. Investment proceeds from the sale and dissolution of his private practice with several equal partners in a Washington law firm had provided a more than adequate windfall. But Marciano couldn't stop practicing law any more than a fish could stop swimming. So with a change in administration at the White House and the appointment of a close friend to Attorney General, Marciano transformed his practice from protecting major corporations from exploitation to going up against those who challenged the law of the land.

"So you view yourself as a crusader?" a member of the press had asked him right after the AG announced his appointment.

"Not at all," he replied with a smile. "I'm simply a concerned citizen."

That had brought a titter from the wall-to-wall bodies packing the press room at the Justice Department and a commendation from his boss on the way he'd handled the questioners in such a suave fashion.

Now entering his third year with the Attorney General, Marciano had made a number of influential friends, not least among them a man he'd truly come to admire and respect: Hal Brognola. Marciano had worked with plenty of federal agents in his time, but he'd never met anyone quite like that one. Brognola had an insight and knowledge into the workings of the criminal underworld like it was nobody's business. Brognola was older—probably much older than he looked— and Marciano had always assumed he was semiretired, since he hardly ever saw the guy. Still, if he needed advice or wanted a fresh approach to a prosecutorial problem, Brognola was the first guy he would go to and that was saying a lot since, to his knowledge, the man had no law degree of any kind other than from the school of hard knocks. Yes, indeed, the guy had been around a *very* long time.

"Honey, I'm leaving!" Marciano called to his wife as he snatched his leather valise off the side table in the entryway of their two-story home.

Caroline had found the place when it got listed with her agency, and while taking a couple through it she fell in love. Marciano liked their private place by a lake in the foothills of the Shenandoah, but the trip had become impractical when his firm grew in size and clientele base, so Caroline convinced him to move to Herndon. He didn't really like the additional upkeep required by the neighborhood association, and he wasn't much for gardening or landscaping, but it did afford him an opportunity to spend quality time with Caroline so he didn't really mind.

Marciano opened the heavy front door of his house and a loud thumping sound greeted him. The steady beat came from some kind of sound system inside the late-model Lincoln SUV with heavy window tinting parked at the curb. Marciano took a couple of hesitant steps through the doorway and closed it securely behind him. As he proceeded down the flagstone pathway that curved toward the driveway where his BMW sat idling, he noticed the rear-seat window of the SUV roll down.

He instantly recognized the object that protruded from the interior, but just a moment too late to really do anything about it.

Gunfire resounded through the chill morning air as a torrent of hot lead spit from the muzzle of the submachine gun. Slugs ripped through Marciano's double-breasted pin-stripe suit and lodged deep in his flesh, his body dancing under the impact of each round. Some of the bullets hit center mass while others grazed him deeply and in enough volume to actually tear chunks of flesh from the bones of his arms and legs. Marciano never saw his shooter; he also never saw the trio of young Hispanic males in gray hooded sweatshirts marked with the symbol of MS-13 as they emerged from the backseat of the SUV.

The young men made their way up the flagstone path, kicked in the front door and fanned out to scour the house. They would complete their work in short order, gunning down Caroline Marciano with the same butchery as her husband and then set fire to the home. These events would signal the fate of the U.S. Attorney General's case, as about the same time police units responded to reports of gunfire coming from the area of the Marciano residence, a federal game warden would discover the butchered remains of a headless and handless victim in a wildlife marshland at the edge of Riverbend Regional Park—remains the coroner took several days to identify as those of Ysidro Perez.

1

Stony Man Farm, Virginia

"Without a case, the AG was forced to release the gang leaders they had in custody," Hal Brognola said. "MS-13 had tried to hide the identity of the body, but fortunately we had DNA and blood samples that had been taken when Perez required medical treatment for his diabetes while in federal custody."

A brooding silence fell on the War Room as the others considered Brognola's grim announcement. Among that group sat a figure more powerful and imposing than all the rest. Arms folded, Mack Bolan leaned back in his chair and stared at the documents of a file folder arrayed before him. Unfortunately, this wasn't a new tune but no question remained in his mind that this particular case required his kind of intervention. No matter the enemy, Bolan's battle plan was always the same— strike terror into the heart of an organization to the point where he destroyed it from the inside out. The time had come to execute that plan against MS-13.

"Tell me more about Marciano," he told Brognola.

The head Fed's eyebrows rose. "You mean beside the fact that he was a top-notch prosecutor and good friend?"

Bolan nodded.

Brognola sighed. "I first met him a few years ago when the AG brought him on board. I haven't known too many like him, Striker. Gary was relentless. He had come from a background in corporate law, but he took to federal prosecution like a duck to water. There are some men who are born for this kind of thing. Just like you were born to do what you do, Gary was the exact same way."

"He never gave you a reason to think he might have been playing for the other team?"

"Absolutely not."

Bolan furrowed his brow. "Then we have to assume these gang members had someone inside the Justice Department feeding them intelligence. They knew where and how to hit Marciano's family, and they knew where this Ysidro Perez had been holed up while he was waiting to testify."

"That was our initial conclusion, as well," Barbara Price interjected.

Stony Man's beautiful mission controller flipped a lock of honey-blond hair behind her ear. Bolan caught the movement and his eyes locked on hers. Through the years, Price had been a steady aid and object of physical comfort to Bolan. They saw each other rarely, but on such occasions they shared a deep connection and intimacy. Price's background in the NSA qualified her better than anyone else to oversee the daily operations of the Stony Man teams, and they appreciated her. But, she had chosen to reserve her deepest and most personal passions for the Executioner.

Brognola continued. "The thing everyone forgets is that I *knew* Gary Marciano. I acted mostly as a sounding board and confidant for him, and one thing I know about him for sure is that he tended to play his cards very close to the vest. In the case of MS-13, there were only two other people who knew those kinds of details—me and the Attorney General. And since my personal questioning of the AG in front of the President leads me to conclude he didn't say anything, the theory that an insider passed sensitive materials to any shot-callers inside MS-13 is damned unlikely."

"There were two other agents with the BATF who questioned Perez," Price said. "I had Bear look deeply into both of these guys, and neither of their activities of recent give us any suspicion they leaked intelligence of their dealings to any outside parties."

"That's right," Aaron "the Bear" added. "I dug into their phone records and e-mails. I even scanned their personal financials for large purchases or cash transactions of any kind. They both came back as clean as a whistle."

That note satisfied Bolan. Kurtzman had repeatedly demonstrated his wizardry in the wide arena of technology. The computer servers installed in the Annex at Stony Man Farm processed and stored massive amounts of information. Kurtzman could hack into just about any secured system in the world. If either of the BATF agents had left a trail of any kind, Kurtzman was the man to find it. If he said they were above reproach, then that was good enough for Bolan.

Price looked toward Brognola, who tendered a curt nod. "Given what we know to this point," she said, "there's only one other possibility. One other person *did* know about Ysidro Perez and Marciano's case. But nobody outside Marciano or Hal knew that. Not even the Attorney General."

"I'm listening," Bolan replied.

"You're familiar with the history of MS-13?" Brognola asked.

Bolan nodded. Mara Salvatrucha Trece's could trace its roots back to the early 1980s and the peasant guerrillas that immigrated into the United States, victims of the bloody civil war in El Salvador. While their origins came about in Los Angeles, they had risen in status and numbers exceeding one hundred thousand members. Their operational territory numbered in excess of thirty states. Their platform: become the largest and most powerful gang in the country; their methods: robbery, gunrunning, drug trafficking and murder-

for-hire. They had become nothing less than a domestic terrorist group, one that was organized and well equipped, and
Bolan knew it was time for him to act in a way law enforcement could not.

"Back in 2001," Price said, "when the FBI first got involved
in this with another witness, this one a pregnant girl who was
also killed by members of the gang, they organized themselves
and conducted major raids in multiple jurisdictions, including areas in Guatemala, Honduras and El Salvador. Because
of how much leadership they took down, the Justice Department thought they had effectively crippled the organization
and its influence. Unfortunately, they were wrong."

"You see, one of the things Gary realized after he was first
assigned Perez's case was that while each cell had its own
shot-callers," Brognola said, "the source of the strings being
pulled was in El Salvador."

"Where the gang originated," Bolan said. "It makes sense.
There's always a bigger fish out there."

"Well, Gary decided the only way they could bring MS-13
down for certain this time was to send an agent to penetrate
the hierarchy. He came to me with his idea, and we agreed
for a time to keep it between just ourselves."

"Why didn't he want to let the AG in on it?" Bolan asked.

Brognola chuckled. "I know why you ask, and I can assure
you now that he didn't suspect his boss of any wrongdoing.
He knew it would be difficult to get the additional funding for
such an operation without any hard proof, so he brought the
guy in from the outside on temporary duty, a BATF agent
named Ignacio Paz. He padded the expense line items and
nobody looked too closely, including the AG, since they knew
he was building a major case against MS-13 with Perez."

"So Paz goes undercover in El Salvador to locate the top
dog in the organization," Bolan concluded.

"Right," Price replied. "And nobody's heard from him in weeks. We have found information on Marciano's computer under some secretly encoded files."

"I've ordered Bear to extract and decrypt the files from the computer so nobody at the AG's office or FBI forensics would find them," Brognola said. "I didn't want to risk exposing Paz. Striker, MS-13 has its own intelligence service. They're in the courts, the police departments, even the jails and prisons. They report on their own members and have even been known to send men out to commit crimes for the sole purpose of circulating them through the prison systems and assassinating deal makers."

"I'm familiar with these kinds of tactics, Hal," Bolan said. "From what you've told me, I think Marciano was on the right track. The only way to put down a group as organized as this is to chop off the head."

"That was our feeling exactly," Brognola replied.

"Okay, I'm in. Where do you want me to begin?"

"Well, Mario Guerra was released yesterday morning," he replied. "As leader of the Hillbangers cell, we believe Herndon's the place to start."

"Your mission has two objectives," Price said as she slid photographs across the table. "First, eliminate the leaders that were released both here and in Los Angeles. If we can't prosecute them because their intelligence unit has managed to stay one step ahead of them, maybe your removing their influence entirely will produce the desired effects. Second, pick up the trail on Ignacio Paz, and if you find him alive get the information you need to destroy the hierarchy in El Salvador."

"I'll need Jack," Boland said. "For at least part of the gig, anyway."

Price smiled. "I figured as much. He's on his way back from a mission with Able Team. They'll be landing here within a few hours."

"Fine. Ask him to be on standby and I'll touch base as soon as I see what's what in Herndon."

"There's one hitch," Brognola said a bit sheepishly. "Since the Justice Department was forced to release Guerra, the AG had to call and inform Herndon's chief of police, a guy named Mike Smalley. Smalley's kind of old school, Striker."

"So what you really mean is he'll be territorial about any federal assistance and try to be in my back pocket every step of the way," Bolan concluded. "I understand."

"Just handle any encounters with kid gloves, okay? The President wants this mission executed surreptitiously. He doesn't like the kind of attention you tend to draw. Not to mention the fact we suspect Herndon's law enforcement will already have its hands full since we're hearing reports the Hillbangers plan to retaliate for Guerra's detainment."

"I'll try to keep it to a dull roar."

BOLAN KNEW his promise would be an empty one.

Stony Man's intelligence was sound wherein it regarded retaliation by MS-13, and the Executioner sensed the imminence of such an attack. He could feel it in his gut. The thing that most bothered him was the intelligence network of which Brognola had spoken. It was big and complex, to be sure, which meant there would be at least a few "officials" on the payroll. Outside of Stony Man, Bolan knew he couldn't trust anybody. Worse yet, this mission ran on the proverbial time clock—a man's life hung in the balance. If the Hillbangers managed to uncover the details of Marciano and his witness, it wouldn't be long before someone discovered evidence of Paz's mission into El Salvador and leaked that intelligence back to the hierarchy. Hence, the mission to eliminate their leadership was more about severing lines of communication than much else.

At least it would buy him some time.

Bolan considered his options of where to start, and since it made perfect sense that the Hillbangers would want to make a statement, he knew the memorial service for Marciano would be the most likely place. Bolan glanced at his watch and realized the service had already started, but he could probably make the outdoor reception scheduled to follow. Bolan took his exit into Herndon off the Dulles Toll Road and drove to a downtown men's shop he remembered.

Forty-five minutes later, the warrior emerged in a midnight blue serge suit, white shirt and pattern-print tie of maroon, blue and teal. The conservative business suit served to provide the look he sought. Except for his height, he didn't think he'd stand out too much at the memorial service. And only the most trained eye would notice the bulge of the Beretta 93-R that rode in shoulder leather beneath his left armpit. Even an expert might miss it, however, since Bolan had long ago perfected the art of role camouflage, and learned how to walk with a gun in a way that eliminated the telltale signs most looked for on any person carrying concealed.

Bolan drove straight to the outdoor area where they were having the memorial service reception, a small park just a few blocks from the Marciano home. The Executioner took note of the two squads he passed through on the road that ran the circumference of the park, as well as the pair of suited agents wearing sunglasses standing post at the park entrance. One waved him down and he complied, rolled down his window and flashed the Justice Department credentials that identified him as a member of the FBI.

The guy studied the creds carefully, gave Bolan a once-over, then nodded and waved him through. Bolan drove on— he was just another federal cop showing up for some free food and to pay his respects, of course. According to Brognola,

Gary Marciano had been a popular man among both his peers and other members of the law-enforcement community. A real friend of cops, Brognola had recalled fondly.

The fact MS-13 would pick this place and time to make its hit might have seemed insane to others—given the sheer number of cops that would be present—but to Bolan it made perfect sense. They would look to make a big and spectacular statement, and wouldn't it be a great bonus if they could take out a few cops in the process? Bolan understood that psyche all too well; he'd seen it more times than he cared to count. MS-13 had stated in no uncertain terms it desired to be the biggest and baddest gang in America, and their target was suburbia because MS-13 probably felt it would prove harder for the police agencies of smaller communities to combat the gang's varied and illicit activities.

Bolan had no such limitations, legal, jurisdictional or otherwise. He would hunt down every last one of them, utterly destroying their organization wherever it reared its ugly head.

Bolan left his car and made his way casually to the group of attendees already ensconced beneath the massive white canopies they had erected over row after row of tables and folding chairs. A small buffet and portable wet bar stood at the end of one of the canopies, attendants hovering over the silver trays from which people served themselves. Just to the left of the entry point of the buffet stood about a dozen well-dressed people greeting the attendees: survivors of the Marciano family. Bolan searched his mental files and immediately recalled the faces of their three children, but he didn't recognize any others. The youngest child stood solemnly between his two older siblings.

Bolan let his gaze rove over the remaining attendees, and he eventually spotted Smalley standing at the table and talking with people. The police chief had shown up dressed in full parade uniform, the gold stars that rode along his collar shimmering almost as if in rhythm with ornate braid on his sleeves and the brim of his cap. Bolan passed over the crowd after a second and marked the faces of several men in suits and sunglasses stationed along the perimeter of the gathering. FBI? BATF or maybe even Secret Service? They didn't carry themselves like plainclothes detectives, although he wouldn't have put it past Smalley to keep a loyal man or two on hand as a bit of insurance.

The conversation seemed a bit solemn and reserved, but the sheer number of voices maintained a steady buzz that seemed to grow in volume as Bolan took in the sights. The Executioner didn't see anything out of the ordinary, so he kept moving along the outskirts of the congregation, careful to maintain a casual demeanor. It wouldn't do to draw anyone's attention, particularly the security team, as long as he had no reason to do so. For now he would blend in and keep one ear open for any conversations that might give him insight into his mission objectives.

Bolan also kept one eye on the family, as the members of MS-13 might feel the job wouldn't be completed until they managed to stamp out every member of Marciano's family. He took special interest in the positions of each man in the security detail, looking for holes or possible weaknesses in their defense. They seemed to have the place pretty well isolated, and unless the gang planned to wade through the crowd and start shooting, it wouldn't make sense for them to attempt the hit.

The most vulnerable part of the layout was the perimeter itself. Bolan had noticed only a couple of squads positioned on the road that circled the park during his drive. There were no other pedestrians—obviously they had sealed off the park for the services—so that removed any risk to bystanders. No, if the attack came it would have to be from the perimeter.

The flash of sunlight on metal caught Bolan's eye, and he turned to see a vehicle approaching from the street where it had entered the rotary. It was big, like a Lincoln or Chrysler, painted dark blue and sporting tinted windows. A second vehicle followed it, an SUV that looked similar to the one described in the police reports Bolan had read from witness statements taken after the Marciano hit.

Both vehicles traveled down the road at a high rate of speed. The sedan stopped just short of the curb with a screech of tires and the SUV wound its way around it, increasing speed and jumping the curb to continue onto the grass. Bolan didn't need any more than that to know he'd called it correctly. He whipped the Beretta from shoulder leather as he dashed from the cover of the tent and charged directly toward a heavy, metal waste container, the fifty-five-gallon drum type, cemented into the ground, with a plastic bag lining its interior.

The Executioner knelt, took up a firing position and prepared to meet his enemy.

Head-on!

2

As the SUV bore down on his position, Bolan moved the selector switch to burst mode, sighted down the slide and took a deep breath.

The vehicle continued on a clear but erratic path in the direction of the clustered canopies. Nobody in the crowd had even seemed to notice the danger yet, which left the Executioner no options. At the rate the truck was closing, it would be on that crowd within fifteen seconds. Bolan's eyes flicked toward the sedan, from which several occupants had emptied, armed with what looked like machine pistols. He marked their positions and then returned his attention to the SUV, steadied his two-handed grip on the pistol and aimed for the driver's side of windshield.

Bolan let out half the breath he'd taken and squeezed the trigger. The windshield spiderwebbed even as Bolan delivered another 3-round burst of 9 mm Parabellum rounds, and that second volley rewarded him with a crimson spray erupting in the interior—a clear sign he'd hit the target. The SUV continued on its straight path and then began to shimmy side-to-side as one of the passengers likely attempted to get control of the wheel.

They had reacted a moment too late, though, as the vehicle jumped a sandy play area and caromed off a heavy wooden merry-go-round. The SUV then jounced across a rough patch of play area, fishtailed through a sandbox and finally hit a triplet of fender-high wooden posts connected with a three-inch-thick rope. The makeshift barrier proved effective enough to bring the vehicle to a halt that rocked the occupants violently into one another.

The Executioner didn't give them a chance to regroup as he burst from cover and charged the vehicle, firing at the SUV on the run. He was careful to remain directly in front of the vehicle, thereby staying clear of the line of fire. The windshield finally collapsed inward, giving Bolan a clear view of the remaining enemy. Bolan assessed the entire situation in a moment.

Driver was down for the count. Ditto for the man seated behind him. Front seat passenger and two remaining backseat occupants were all moving. Bolan slowed as he got near, dropped the pistol's magazine for a new one and opened up with a fresh salvo. The men in the SUV could do only two things—panic and die—as the Executioner unleashed a fusillade of vengeance on them. Bolan triggered his weapon repeatedly, catching the front seat passenger first as he presented the most immediate threat in bringing his submachine gun to bear. Bolan's 3-round burst split the gangster's skull wide open and added to the bloodstained décor of the SUV interior. Another died with two rounds to the chest and a third to the throat.

The lone survivor managed to pull himself together enough to bail from the SUV, but he didn't get far. As he leveled his SMG in Bolan's direction, the Executioner got him with twin rounds through his right thigh. The gunner twisted away and his weapon flew from his grasp, arcing through the air and skittering across the wet grass on impact, well out of his grip. He began to writhe on the ground, holding his wounded leg, and Bolan knew he was no longer a threat. The locals could take him into custody for questioning.

Bolan heard the tap-tap-tap of the machine pistols and semiauto guns being fired at him, but from that distance the gunners from the sedan were unlikely to hit him. Bolan heard shouts and turned to see the security detail along with about a half-dozen uniforms reacting to the scene, several with pistols drawn and rushing toward him. It was time to take his leave. Bolan turned and sprinted toward the parking lot where he'd left his car. He had a slim chance of catching the gangsters in the sedan who were still plinking at him with only futile results.

Bolan had nearly reached his car when two plainclothes security officers attempted to stop him. He flashed the badge as he reached the vehicle, disengaged the door locks with the keyless remote and jumped behind the wheel. The two men slid to a halt and watched helplessly as Bolan cranked the engine, dropped into Reverse and backed out of the lot with a spew of dust and gravel from his tires. Bolan continued in reverse until his wheels found pavement and then executed a J-turn that swung the nose of Stony Man's loaner vehicle in the direction he'd been backing.

The V8 engine of the Mustang GT roared beneath the hood as Bolan slammed the stick into Second gear and blasted out of the lot with a squeal of tires. The Mustang accelerated and Bolan smoothly shifted into Third gear, then Fourth, heading along the circular road that would connect him with the sedan crew. He had no doubt these were Guerra's people. They didn't operate like professional hitters. They had intended to do a drive-by on the mourners at the park, plain and simple. Bolan was thankful nobody else had been at the park, particularly children playing in the area of his conflagration with the men in the SUV.

Bolan looked toward the sedan just as it executed a tight turnaround and headed the way it had come. The Executioner increased his speed, determined not to let them get away. He checked his rearview mirror and saw the frantic scrambling of police toward their cars. There was no longer a threat at the park; the threat was now wherever Bolan allowed Guerra's men to lead him. Surely they would know he was following them, and he couldn't say he really minded. Inside the large, nylon bag on the seat next to him was an arsenal of assorted weapons for making war.

In addition to the Beretta, Bolan had brought along his .44 Magnum Desert Eagle, the standard hand cannon for dispatching bad guys. It was especially handy when he needed decent firepower in a close-quarters situation where automatic weapons would be clumsy and awkward. He'd also procured an MP-5 K machine pistol, an FNC assault rifle by Fabrique Nationale and a dozen or so M-67 hand grenades. In the trunk he carried some additions to round out his rolling armory, which he would bring into use as the occasions arose.

Bolan tried to coax some more speed from the Mustang, slowing only enough to make the curve at the park exit without flipping the high-performance sports car. The sedan hadn't gone very far and Bolan knew he wouldn't have trouble catching up. He grit his teeth when flashing lights of several police squads suddenly rounded the corner of a street farther up and headed directly for the fleeing vehicle. Bolan wished he had a police radio so he could warn them the suspects were heavily armed, but he knew it wouldn't do any good. If the profile on Smalley was even remotely accurate, Herndon would put every available resource at law enforcement's disposal to make sure there was no further bloodshed by MS-13, and Smalley's men probably wouldn't be too careful or discriminate about how they did that. Such a fact would only lead to more good men and women dying, this time men and women wearing badges.

Bolan watched helplessly as the sedan ground to a halt and flashes from muzzles protruding from the windows chopped the glass and metal of the squad cars to shreds. One of the squads was still far enough back to escape the onslaught, but the closest two didn't fare well. While the police were trained to respond to such incidents, they were hardly equipped to go up against fanatic gangbangers armed with machine guns and assault rifles.

On the other hand, Bolan was.

The Executioner raced toward the carnage and slammed on his brakes at the last moment, swinging his vehicle around the outside of the sedan as he reached into the bag and withdrew the MP-5 K. None of the sedan's occupants had even noticed him, as they were still focused on shooting up the police vehicles. Bolan put the weapon in battery, lowered his window and stuck his left arm out, machine gun in hand. He depressed the trigger and swept the vehicle. The front and rear windows of what the soldier could now see was a Lincoln MKZ shattered under the attack. The bodies of the gunners danced under the massive assault. He yanked an M-67 high explosive grenade and thumbed away the spoon as he raked the sedan. Amid the shouts and curses of those who survived his barrage, Bolan tossed the grenade casually into the interior and then put the Mustang into Reverse and backed away.

The superheated ball of gas filled the interior compartment a moment later, and flames belched from all four window frames. The blast produced enough effect to lift the car an inch or two off its wheels and settle it back to the pavement in a roaring crash. Bolan could feel the heat and shock wave of the explosion pass through the front window of the Mustang, setting his teeth on edge. He shielded his eyes in order not to be blinded by the flash effect of the PETN-fed blast.

"So much for a dull roar," Bolan muttered to himself.

The Executioner pulled the Mustang to the curb a safe distance from the flaming wreckage of the sedan, burst from his car and rushed to see if he could render aid to any of the

wounded officers. For now, he had evened the score between
MS-13 and the Marcianos. That would teach Mario Guerra a
lesson—make him realize he and his Hillbangers weren't
quite as invincible as they thought. And there was one other
thing Guerra would learn very soon.

Bolan was just getting started.

"YOU WANT TO TELL ME just what the hell you thought you
were doing, Cooper?" a red-faced Mike Smalley asked. "This
is a Herndon police matter, and the Herndon Police will
handle it!"

"No, that's where you're mistaken, Chief," Bolan replied
calmly. "This is a matter for everyone."

"Is it now? Okay then—" Smalley leaned forward in his
chair and snatched a sheet of paper off the edge of his desk,
placing it in front of him "—let's just see what we have here.
I had the contents of that sports car out there inventoried. I
hope you don't mind."

"I do," Bolan replied coolly. "You have no right or jurisdiction to search my vehicle."

Smalley looked at Bolan and raised his eyebrows. "I don't?
Well, that's funny because I'm almost positive the search
warrant I acquired from a D.C. judge just a little while ago
said I did." He turned his attention back to the paper. "So let's
see, where was I? Oh, yes, here we go. One semiautomatic
.44 Magnum handgun with no registration record, one 5.56 mm
assault rifle of foreign make, one M-16 A-2 assault rifle with
M-203 grenade launcher in the trunk, and about one hundred
pounds of varied ordnance, military grade."

Smalley locked eyes with Bolan. "Automatic weapons that
aren't government issued? Military explosives? Just who the
hell *are* you exactly, Cooper—if that's even your real name?
Who do you work for? And don't hand me any more bullshit

about how you're with the Justice Department. Those creds you're carrying are a little too clean for my tastes."

Bolan had been as polite as possible to this point, but Smalley had gone too far now, and the time for niceties was over. Beside, the cat was out of the bag, and he didn't have any more time to be cheeky. Brognola had said Smalley was old school, which simply meant he was only willing to play hardball with those who were adept at giving back as good as they got. So it was time to change tact.

"All right, Chief," Bolan said, feigning frustration. "You want the truth, the gloves come off. Quite simply, I'm operating with the full cooperation of the Oval Office. You understand? I don't answer to you or frankly to anyone else. Gary Marciano's family and witness were killed because MS-13 has become an epidemic in this country. One I've been sent to cure. They warned me you were hard-nosed and by-the-book, which I don't have any problem with. But my mission is to eradicate this threat to the American public once and for all. Now you're either into that and willing to cooperate or you're not. Either way, I don't really care because I have a job to do, and I'm going to do it. I could have you removed from that chair with one phone call. I'm not interested in doing that, so you'd better decide now if you stand a better chance of focusing on protecting the people of Herndon or standing in my way, all for the sake of protecting your ego."

Smalley's face reddened, and the veins bulged from his neck and forehead. His apoplexy at Bolan's words was obvious, but the soldier also knew Smalley realized he was telling the truth. Herndon was its own municipal entity, to be certain, but it fell under the direct influence of Washington, D.C.—just as all the rest of the capital's neighboring communities. Smalley served at the pleasure of the mayoral appointment, and the mayor wouldn't dare refuse a presidential "suggestion" if it came down to it. Still, Bolan liked Smalley for the very reasons Brognola had cautioned him about the police chief, and preferred to have the guy's cooperation.

Smalley finally calmed down and nodded. "All right, Cooper. You've been straight with me, and I guess that's the best I can ask of any man. And I suppose we owe you a debt, since you saved the lives of a number of cops. Hell, we ought to give you the key to the city for *that*. But this is still my hometown, understand that. I took an oath to uphold the laws here, and I don't need some Delta Force cowboy or whatever you are running around this city shooting and blowing up everything in sight."

"You'll find I'm a cautious man, Smalley," Bolan replied easily. "I don't hit until I'm confident the innocents are well out of the line of fire."

Smalley shrugged and threw up his hands. "And?"

"And that's where you come in," Bolan said. "This is *your* town, just as you say. So I believe you have a pretty good idea where MS-13 conducts its operations, and the best way to find this Mario Guerra."

Smalley snorted with a scowl. "Guerra. Yes, he's a real piece of work that guy. I know he's personally responsible for at least a dozen crimes, including rape, robbery and murder. I just can't prove it."

"You won't have to prove it," Bolan said. "The best thing you and your men can do for me is to round up as many of his posse as you can find and keep them on ice. Twenty-four hours, that's all I'm asking for."

"Okay…fine, sure, I can do that. But I don't see how that's going to help you capture Guerra, or build a case against him that will stick."

"Building a case against him isn't my mission objective," Bolan said.

"Then what do you plan to do?"

The Executioner remained silent, but the cock of his head and steely gaze served as an adequate answer to Smalley's question.

"I see," Smalley said.

"Sometimes we can't play by the rules with a group like MS-13. They've terrorized this country long enough, Chief. It's time for real action, permanent action."

Smalley nodded slowly with a faraway expression, not even meeting Bolan's gaze. He could tell the policeman was warring with the idea just presented to him. In the most technical sense, Bolan's tactics were nothing short of military operations conducted in the civilian sector, a clear violation of a dozen or so federal laws, including one constitutional amendment. Unfortunately, the breaking of such laws was sometimes the only way to combat those who chose to operate outside them. Still, for a guy like Chief Michael Vernon Smalley, it was a damned anachronism to the end purposes of law enforcement and contradictory to everything he knew.

"Though I don't necessarily agree with your approach," Smalley said, "I promise you'll have my support during your efforts."

"That's all I would ever ask of you or anyone," Bolan replied.

"Okay, so how do we do this?"

"First, I need some idea of the core operations area for MS-13."

Smalley nodded, rose and went to a map of the city hanging on the wall to his right. He pointed to a small area on the south side of the city where it bordered a major road. Smalley traced his finger along that road and said, "This is the Dulles Toll Road, which also marks the border between the city and unincorporated areas of Herndon and Reston. Most of the gang activity has been confined to this region. One of the problems we've faced in recent times is the influx of illegal immigrants to this area. We don't really know why that's the case, but we *do* know it's taxed many of our resources. When we first started to have problems with MS-13 and related gang activity, the Justice Department formed the Northern Virginia Gang Task Force—then NVGTF. There are sixteen communities and law-enforcement agencies now directly involved with the organization, and since 2003 we've accomplished much in the cleanup."

"And then recently you were flooded with a resurgence of activity?" Bolan asked.

Smalley nodded and dropped back into his chair. "Right. We think it's directly related to the fact we've been dealing with this illegal immigration problem. There's no way for us to combat both problems, and the task force has been suffering from monetary cutbacks since we *thought* we had the problem licked."

"Okay. It sounds like the south's the place for me to start. One other question, though."

"Shoot."

"Did you know anything about the case Gary Marciano was building against MS-13 or this witness he had stashed away?"

Smalley shook his head. "I knew Gary Marciano pretty well. Naturally, he was a prominent member of this community. You see, the Town of Herndon numbers about twenty-two thousand people, but we've always tried to maintain that sense of a small community. I considered Gary a personal friend, but I didn't know he was working on a major case. If I had, I might have offered him some protection or assistance. Lord knows, he helped out this department on many occasions. He'll be missed, though, and you can bet your ass that his family will receive all the resources at my disposal for the future. Whatever they need, they'll get. I put my personal stamp of guarantee all over that one."

Bolan nodded as he rose and stuck out his hand. "I'm sure you will. I appreciate the help, Chief."

Smalley shook the Executioner's hand and said, "You'll stay in touch?"

"Count on it."

As Bolan turned to leave the chief's office, Smalley called after him. "Hey, Cooper?"

"Yeah."

"You really think you can fix this problem of ours?"

"I can't make any promises," the warrior replied. "But in twenty-four hours when the smoke clears and you see who's left standing, you'll have your answer."

3

"Who is this *pinche,* homeboys, eh?" Mario Guerra splayed out on the sofa with a forty-ounce bottle of beer in his left hand, banged his right fist against his chest and flashed the younger men surrounding him with a sign of solidarity. "Who is this *pinche cabrón* you allow to kill our homeboys and dis the one-three?"

"We don't know who he is, Mario," replied Louie Maragos, one of Guerra's lieutenants.

Guerra sneered. "Well, then, you better find out, homeboys. You know what I'm saying? This dude, he kills like what… nine boys?"

"Ten," another soldier corrected.

"Shut the fuck up!" Guerra said, tossing his half-full beer bottle at the man. "I want to know who he is and how he knew we were going to show up."

"We can find all that out, *jefe,*" Maragos replied. "But how do we find out how he knew about our plans to hit the park?"

"What, you some kind of clown or something?" Guerra asked. "Obviously, we still got a snitch on the inside somewhere. We got someone who likes to run their mouth—" he flapped his thumb against his fingers "—the minute that they see a cop. It means that somebody probably had to be helping Ysidro. Maybe it's even one of *you* homeboys."

Maragos bristled at the suggestion. "Hey, listen, homeboy, I know you're in charge and all, but there ain't no way I'm

going to let you accuse me of something without some proof."
Maragos dropped his hand to where he could easily reach the
piece he kept at the small of his back. "Ain't *no* way, *jefe. Sí?*"

"Okay, okay," Guerra said. He sat back down and shook
his head. "I ain't going to accuse you of nothing. I wasn't
going to do that, homeboy."

Maragos nodded and relaxed his hand. There were rules in
the organization; it was a necessity for the kind of place it was.
Every moment a homeboy had to be looking over his shoulder,
watching not only for trouble from outsiders but from within
the organization. Every member had to prove himself in a
grueling initiation that included not only a thirteen second
beat down by other members, but also by doing something to
prove his loyalty. For the females it might be just taking a beat
down, or maybe having sex with a number of the ranking
vatos. In other cases it might be doing a strong-arm robbery,
selling drugs or even participating in a hit with other members.

Whatever the case, the motto of the gang was simple:
Being in MS-13 Will Land You in the Cemetery, the Hospital
or Prison. The rules were designed to enhance solidarity and
prevent a breakdown in the structure of the gang. This code
of conduct included rules for how to deal with defectors and
dissidents, rules like "you rat, you die" and "everything
belongs to the gang," and the context of those rules made it
just as serious an infraction to accuse someone of being un-
faithful to MS-13 without proof, simply because the penal-
ties for betrayal were so severe. It was their code, their creed,
and nobody—not even a shot-caller—was above the rules.

"Do any of you homeboys have any idea where this guy
came from? Who he's working for?" Guerra asked more calmly.

"My informant says he might be working with the *fede-
rales,*" Maragos replied. "He might also be a local on loan
from the Virgins."

Guerra smiled at their own internal reference to the gang task force of the state, a unit that had been the bane of the Hill-bangers' existence since its formation. After the death of the traitor in 2001 and subsequent imprisonment of the leader who ordered her execution, Guerra had taken over as shot-caller for the Hillbangers. He ordered them to lie low and let enough time pass so that the task force became convinced it had made a difference. In the meantime, the MS-13 had opened up a brand-new operation—alien smuggling from regions all over Central America. This endeavor had become quite lucrative while they moved drug running and robbery to the status of "last resort," a sort of subset of secondary operations due to the increased risk since the Virgins started cracking down on them.

"I don't think so," Guerra finally said. "That limp dick, Smalley, doesn't have the guts to come face-to-face with us. He has to be from the Feds."

"This *chingada* is dangerous, *jefe,*" said Jocoté Barillas, another lieutenant. "He uses bombs and machine guns."

Guerra stood, walked to Barillas and gently patted the side of his face with a sardonic chuckle. He then looked at each of them as he said, "So do we. I want you to find this man, you got me? You find him and you bury him. Otherwise, you'll have to contend with Le Gango Jefe, *sí?*"

Yes, they understood the threat all too well. Every shot-caller was the leader of his particular unit and any territory they covered. But they in turn answered to the Leader of the Gang—in this case, the nameless entity who controlled every last bit of action from his headquarters in El Salvador. A multijurisdictional force of law agents had attempted many times to bring down Le Gango Jefe, and each time they had failed. Nobody in MS-13, anywhere in the world, operated without this man's approval. Mara Salvatrucha Trece's ultimate goal was to be the largest and most powerful gang in the world. That took more than just whipping up a bunch of *vatos* to do business and pledge their loyalty. It took organization and planning, and that's what Le Gango Jefe brought to the table.

As a shot-caller, every one of Guerra's lieutenants knew he had a direct access to the top man. They also knew it wouldn't bode well for any of them if Guerra had to make a phone call to this man and tell him they had failed in their mission to bring down the *federale* who had killed ten of their homeboys. Ultimately, Guerra was trying to help them by making it clear that it would look much better for them all if they handled this problem internally with local resources before it got out of control.

"I don't care what you have to do, homeboys, I want you to bring him down. And do it now."

"Okay, Mario, we'll find him," Maragos promised.

"Then why are you still here?" he said, clapping his hands and then jerking both thumbs toward the door. "Come on, *essás. Vámonos!*"

Each acknowledged him with the standard gang sign that spelled out MS-13 and then hit the door in a hurry. He watched them go out and then went to the fridge and pulled a fresh beer from the stash there. He took a long pull from the forty-ounce bottle and then looked out his tenement window onto the dusky cityscape. Somewhere out there, he knew, the enemy was searching for him. He'd narrowly escaped confinement for life in prison, and while such things were a part of the risk he took, the idea of spending his youth behind concrete walls and steel bars didn't hold much appeal.

He needed to keep a cool head and plan his next move. They needed to find this cop or special agent and do him right. He'd spilled the blood of ten homeboys, soldiers operating under Guerra's orders, and with that single action this *pinche* had signed his own death warrant. Maragos was good, one of the best, really. He would find the man and do what needed to be done. And then Guerra could bring his son and wife out here where they would be safe. He would be able to protect them here then.

And then he could begin to put his plan in motion. A plan to rule all of the East Coast—a plan to rule a society.

AFTER BOLAN LEFT police headquarters, he drove straight to the MS-13 key operations area Smalley had pointed out to him and booked a room in a run-down motel just two miles south of Dulles Toll Road. The elderly toothless Hispanic woman behind the grimy counter in the motel office had been quite pleased to take Bolan's nice, crisp hundred-dollar bill for his two-night stay—especially when he advised her to keep the change.

Once the Executioner had settled in, he attached an anti-listening device to the phone and then dialed a long number from memory. There were three beeps, a signal the connection had been rerouted and secured from any type of bugging or other electronic surveillance technologies, and then Aaron Kurtzman's voice came over the line.

"How's it going?" Kurtzman said.

"I started with a real bang," Bolan quipped.

"Well, your man Jack's been here for a couple of hours now, chomping at the bit. You want to talk to him?"

"Sure."

"What's shaking, Sarge?" Jack Grimaldi's voice greeted him. Grimaldi was Stony Man's ace pilot and a Bolan ally.

"Hey, Jack," Bolan replied. "Thanks for being on standby. I know you just got back from a mission."

"Hey! You know I'm always ready to fly a mission for you, Sarge. You keep things interesting."

"Don't I. Hal gave you the rundown of the mission parameters?"

"He did," Grimaldi said. "I imagined you had your hands full right at the moment, so I figured to get a couple hours' sleep before heading to Dulles. I'll be ready by the time you want to leave for Los Angeles."

"You read my mind, ace. I'll call when I'm on my way there."

"Understood. Okay, Hal and Barb are waiting in the ops center for you, so I'll transfer you now."

The men said their goodbyes, and then Brognola's voice came on a moment later. "What happened to that dull roar?"

Bolan couldn't see Brognola's expression, but the kidding tone caused him to receive the statement as nothing more than a good-natured jibe. "I only blew up one car."

Brognola laughed. "That is pretty mild in comparison to most of your fireworks displays."

"Agreed. I'm sorry to report Mario Guerra wasn't among them, but then I wouldn't expect a weasel like that to get his own hands dirty."

"We heard about your run-in with Smalley," Price said. "You need us to run some interference?"

"No, we're good. Smalley's actually not difficult to handle once you get to talking with the guy. Basically he wants the same thing we do."

"Peace in the valley?"

"Right."

"What about the increased gang activity of late?" Brognola asked. "Did he have any explanations?"

"It looks like a matter of sheer numbers. This Northern Virginia Gang Task Force has lost much of the funding they had early on, which tells me once the crackdown started MS-13 chilled out until some of the heat was off. He also said they've had a big influx of illegal immigrants into the area lately."

"What's lately?" Price inquired.

"Last couple of years or so," Bolan replied. "My guess is that MS-13 has something to do with that, as well."

"You think it's a diversionary tactic?" Brognola asked.

"Possibly, Hal, although I wouldn't put it past them to use it as a way of subsidizing their more illicit activities. There's been more focus on illegal immigration down on the border than in any other part of the country. If they flood the market with the poor and hungry masses, they can effectively choke the resources of the system. Before the government knows it, it's got an epidemic on its hands with insufficient resources to combat such a disaster."

"And under the scramble and panic, MS-13 can get busy once again with little interference," Brognola concluded. "And the increased criminal activity would be blamed on the immigration problem."

"Exactly."

"It's ingenious," Price stated.

"Which tells me Marciano's theory about someone calling the shots in El Salvador has merit. In fact, I'd be interested to know how many of the immigrants that have been detained by INS or incarcerated for criminal activity are from that region."

"We can get Aaron and Barb on that pronto," Brognola said.

"We'll get started on it right away," Price said. "Take care of yourself, Striker."

"Wilco," Bolan replied and then continued, "Hal, you might want to pull some strings and see what you can do about getting additional protection assigned to Marciano's kids. If MS-13 tried to hit them once, they'll try again and I don't think Smalley has the manpower or resources to do an effective job of security with all the other things weighing him down right now."

"I'll make it happen," Brognola assured him. "What else do you need?"

"That's it for now. There's no rush on the intelligence data regarding the immigration problem here. I've picked up some good leads from Smalley about Guerra's area of operation here, and now I'm going to blitz them and see what I can churn up. Smalley's agreed to run interference for me in the meantime, take some of the smaller piles off the streets so I can follow the trail of leftovers back to Guerra."

"Fair enough," Brognola replied. "We'll get things happening at this end, and I'll inform the Man you're on the path to taking care of business."

"Roger. Out here."

Bolan disconnected the call and then set about the task of checking his equipment. Smalley had released the weapons and ordnance back to him without a fight, since his warrant only blanketed him for a search and a number of interagency memorandums of understanding precluded him from seizing anything he found.

Bolan stripped out of his dress clothes into a different kind of suit, one he knew to be most appropriate for the activities he planned over the next twenty-four hours. The skintight blacksuit and combat boots transformed the Executioner into an imposing figure. A military web belt encircled his waist, held in place by a pair of load-bearing suspenders. Various implements of war dangled from the harness, including the .44 Magnum Desert Eagle in a hip holster, a garrote, Ka-Bar fighting knife and several M-67 fragmentation grenades. The Beretta 93-R nestled in a shoulder rig, and ammo pouches along the belt with magazines of 9 mm ammo completed the ensemble.

Bolan packed the rest of his belongings into the waterproof equipment bag, which he stowed in the trunk of the Mustang. He climbed behind the wheel—a tight squeeze given all the gear he wore—and then headed for a tavern that the intelligence computers of the NVGTF had advised had a back room where MS-13 conducted illegal gambling operations and sold narcotics.

The Executioner was headed into the den of troublemakers, and he planned to collect a debt.

In full.

4

Bolan seemed like a ghostly specter as he passed through the doorway of the tavern and walked calmly across the grimy floor headed directly for a back door marked Fire Exit ONLY!

Most of the patrons were seated at the door with their backs to him and so, under the din of happy hour, didn't even notice the wraithlike form that moved past them with instruments of war dangling from every part of its imposing form. The bartender noticed, however, and reached beneath the bar to sound an alarm with one hand while using the other to scoop up a shotgun. Bolan saw the move in his peripheral vision.

In fact, he'd half expected it.

The Executioner whirled to face the threat as he reached for the Desert Eagle at his hip. He leveled the pistol at the bartender's chest just as the guy brought his shotgun to bear. Bolan waited until he saw the bartender quickly jack the wooden pump on the gun, heard the clack as the motion fed a 12-gauge shell into the breech, before he steadied the muzzle on his target and squeezed the trigger. The slug left the pistol at a muzzle velocity of over 1,300 feet per second. The round punched through the bartender's sternum, cracked the breastbone, tore out his lower airway and blew out a part of his spine. The impact sent him crashing into the neat row of bottles behind him as he triggered a harmless round into the ceiling.

Pandemonium erupted inside the bar, with half the patrons dropping to the floor and the other half drawing knives or guns and searching for cover. Bolan didn't wait to become a target for an overanxious shooter, instead putting his foot to the alleged fire exit door, a scenario he knew to be unlikely, since there was no safety bar or alarm visible. His intuition paid off as the door gave way to his imposing frame.

While the reaction of the gangbanger security force proved admirable, it wasn't a match for the Executioner—he had surprise on his side.

Bolan took the closest target, a hood in a gray sweatshirt toting a machine pistol, and blew his skull apart with a double tap at the same moment he reached for a grenade on his LBE harness. Bolan found cover behind a large support pole as two other MS-13 soldiers opened on his position with Ingram MAC-10s. Their possession of such arcane weaponry surprised him but he filed it away for later consideration and primed his grenade. He let the spoon fly and counted three seconds of cook-off time before breaking cover and lobbing the bomb in the direction of the enemy gunners. The grenade exploded in midair, giving neither youth time to find cover. The shock wave from the high explosive charge separated an arm and head from one of the gangbangers while the other suffered a mouthful of fractured teeth and third degree burns across most of his upper body.

Bolan swept the muzzle of the Desert Eagle the breadth of the room and tracked on a fourth man who had escaped the full effect of the grenade. The gangbanger looked to be vying for a better position where he could flank Bolan but the room was sealed up tight as a drum, and he had nowhere to go. The crowd that had been inside gambling now rushed past Bolan and headed for the exit door. The Executioner ignored them, focused on neutralizing the threat at hand. The MS-13 gunner leveled his machine pistol at Bolan, but the soldier took him with a single round to the shoulder before the man got a shot off. The impact ripped a large hole through the meaty portion and knocked the weapon loose from the man's grip.

Bolan swept the room once more with the smoking pistol but no further threats greeted him. He crossed the room where tables were overturned. Chips, cash, liquor and smoldering cigarettes had been strewed across the floor. Bolan vaulted the one table an MS-13 gangster had overturned and aimed the pistol point-blank at the surviving gunner's forehead. He looked more like a kid than a grown man, with his acne-covered face and full head of slicked back hair, but Bolan marked him in his early twenties; yeah, definitely old enough to know better. He rolled on the floor, one hand covering his wounded shoulder, the blood oozing through his fingers and soaking his shirt sleeve as it left smudges on the floor around him.

"I have two questions for you," Bolan said. "Answer them both truthfully and you live. Understand?"

The kid merely nodded.

"Question one. You work for Mario Guerra?"

"*Sí*...yes."

"Good. Second question, did he order the hit on Gary Marciano?"

This time the kid said nothing. Bolan knew about the rules in the gang, that the penalty for informing on the gang with the cops was death. Frankly, Bolan didn't see much difference from this kid's point of view. If he ratted them out, they would surely hunt him down and kill him, and if he didn't speak he was taking the chance Bolan would put a bullet through his head. While he might believe the latter or not, he could be *certain* that his homeys would kill him if he betrayed the code of silence.

"Check that," Bolan said. "That's not a fair question, so let's try a different one. Suppose I wanted to buy some drugs. Where would I look?"

"Y-you don't want to buy drugs."

"Maybe, maybe not," Bolan replied. "But let's just pretend that I do for a moment. Let's say that I'm not asking you to give up anything you wouldn't give up to some pimp or prostitute or coked up vagrant on the street. Right? Telling me where I can get some drugs isn't giving anything up. You'd tell one of them, so you can tell me."

"My homeboys will kill me if I say anything to you, man."

Bolan put the hot muzzle of the gun against the kid's cheek and kicked the kid's hand away and stepped on his shoulder. "Let's try it again. Where?"

The young man produced a blood-curdling scream and Bolan eased off the pressure. "Okay…okay!" the kid said between labored breaths. "Place is called Tres Hermanos, down on the strip east of here, borders Reston. It's there…it's there where you can buy. Now please, please stop!"

Bolan nodded and took his foot off the kid's shoulder. He then reached to a medical pouch on his harness, withdrew a compress with bandage from it, tore open the thick paper wrapping with his teeth and quickly dressed the youth's wound. He then stripped the kid of belt and shoes, checked him for any hidden weapons and then cleared out of there. Back in the main bar area, all the patrons had vacated the place and Bolan could hear sirens in the distance. He checked his watch, deciding not to hit the club right away. He wanted to give the cops a little time to catch up. For now, he would get a quick bite and then go visit this Tres Hermanos, see what kind of flies he could attract to the web.

The war had begun and time—for Mario Guerra—was running out.

BOLAN JUST FINISHED the last bite of his meal when the cellular phone on the seat next to him rang.

The Executioner wiped his fingers on a napkin before growling a short greeting into the receiver.

"Cooper, it's Smalley," the chief replied.

"Yeah."

"I thought we had a deal, pal."

"And what was that?"

"I thought you weren't going to start shooting up my town."

"I never said that," Bolan replied. "And besides, it was only one rat hole I shot up in your town. I'm sure nobody will miss the business. You found my little greeting card?"

"The wounded banger?"

"That's the one."

"I did," Smalley said. He let out a sigh and added, "But he lawyered up as soon as we read him his rights, so I don't think he's going to be talking to us any time soon."

"I didn't have any trouble getting the information I wanted from him."

"Yeah, we heard all about that. First from the punk, then his attorney, and probably from the ACLU and a half-dozen other agencies in time for the early-morning edition of the *Washington Post*."

"I needed to confirm a couple tidbits of intelligence and he was happy to cooperate," Bolan said. "Now if you're done, I have some new information. That Hillbanger admitted he was operating under orders from Mario Guerra. He also gave up the main location of this drug operation they've been running. And I ran your immigration problem by my own people. We think we've got a logical argument that the increased illegal immigrants are actually a pipeline opened by some heavy hitters overseeing MS-13 operations all through this country. I believe they've been using the pipeline to divert your attention away from their other activities."

"In other words, you think they've been just waiting us out," Smalley concluded.

"You nailed it."

"Damn! I can't believe we would have fallen for something like that!"

"Don't beat up on yourself too much, Smalley," Bolan replied easily. "There wasn't any way you could've known, and even if you did, there was even less you could do about it. That whole thing falls into INS's lap, and whoever's overseeing MS-13 operations at the national level knows how bureaucratically mired that agency is."

"So you really think there's an overboss in this," Smalley said matter-of-factly. "Like some kind of godfather of the Mara Salvatrucha?"

"I don't know for sure yet, but I have some evidence from an operation Marciano was running under the table that strongly suggests it."

"So now what?"

"Now," Bolan said, his eyes returning to the restaurant's entrance, "I follow up this lead the Hillbanger gave me on the drug operation. I'm betting it will take me directly to where Mario Guerra's holed up."

"Well, I've started deploying every available man to sweep the neighborhoods and get as many Hillbangers off the streets as possible."

"Did you get anything from the first prisoner I took from the hit at the park this afternoon?"

"He's still in recovery from the surgery. That shot did some major damage to his leg. In fact, doctors say he might lose it altogether. Apparently there was a lot of nerve damage and it was difficult to repair."

"Wish I could feel bad, but I don't," Bolan replied.

"I'm sure," Smalley said. "We're not shedding any tears,

either. We've had him up on charges a number of times, but he always managed to beat the rap. Guess he's not bullet-proof, though."

"They usually aren't."

"All right, Cooper, I got to go. But just keep in mind that my men are out there trying to help you, so try not to accidentally shoot one of them."

"Like I said, I'm very cautious. Just keep them away from Tres Hermanos for the next hour."

Bolan killed the call and returned his full attention to the scene before him. While talking to Smalley, he'd watched a number of vehicles park in the lot and produce occupants who didn't appear to be anything more than legitimate patrons. The Executioner knew looks could be deceiving, and he'd begun to wonder if the MS-13 gangster had sent him on a wild-goose chase, yet something in his gut told him to wait it out. If the restaurant did serve as a front to their drug sales operations, it wasn't like they would go about advertising the fact to the casual observer.

As if on cue, Bolan observed a late model BMW pull to the curb in front of the entrance and drop off two men seated in the back. Both of them were dressed in nice clothes and wore lots of jewelry—the dark sunglasses seemed particularly strange for the time of evening. The BMW's driver then pulled away and turned into the lot to wait while the pair of tough-looking customers made their way inside.

Bingo.

The Executioner left the Mustang he'd parked across the street and approached the BMW waiting in its blind spot. When he'd gone half the distance, he saw a spark and flicker through the back window. A moment later, the driver stuck his hand out the side and Bolan could just make out the pinpoint glow of a cigarette cherry. The soldier continued

toward the BMW until he was within a few feet and drew the
Beretta from shoulder leather. He reached out and grabbed the
driver's wrist while simultaneously sliding his gun hand under
the man's triceps and pulling backward, using the arm as a
lever for which he could quite effectively control the driver.

"Whadda—" the man started.

Bolan twisted until he had the man's arm locked tightly
against his abdomen and laid the muzzle of the Beretta against
his left cheek. "Drop the smoke."

He complied.

"The two you dropped just now," Bolan said. "Who are they?"

"No way, man," the driver replied in a thick, Hispanic
accent. "I ain't no rat."

"You're right, that would be an insult to rodents." Bolan
pressed back on the arm and put the muzzle tighter against
the driver's cheek. "But since you're not going to talk, I have
no further use for you."

"Wait, wait!" The driver's breath came quickly now, obviously keyed in to the implicit threat of Bolan's actions.
"They're just collectors. They just work for the boss. We all
work for the boss."

"Mario Guerra?" The man kept silent and Bolan tapped
him with the Beretta. "I asked a question. Guerra?"

"Yeah, yeah," the young man replied. "Guerra."

"Thanks," Bolan said.

The warrior then drove an elbow into the soft point behind
the driver's ear, knocking him out cold. His body slumped
forward against the steering wheel. Bolan reached around his
inert form and killed the engine. He removed the keys and
tossed them over a nearby wooden fence that bordered the
parking lot, then proceeded casually to the entrance of the restaurant. Just like the tavern, he didn't have a lot of time for
pleasantries. He'd hit the place fast and hard in order to keep

Guerra off guard. That was the tactic he'd chosen to employ: push the enemy, keep him reeling until he made a mistake and exposed himself.

Bolan knew Guerra couldn't hide behind his gang forever, and Guerra likely knew Bolan knew this.

The Executioner intended to send Guerra a message and remove any doubt in the shot-caller's mind, first with his assault on the illegal bookmaking operation and now by shutting down their main distribution pipeline. Bolan crossed the threshold of the restaurant and a big man in a dark suit, standing behind a reservation podium, accosted the warrior by putting a beefy hand on his shoulder. This wasn't just any maître d', not in a family Mexican restaurant in the barrio of Herndon, Virginia—especially not one that doled out drugs as one of its entrées.

Bolan reacted with the blinding speed that belied years of experience as a combat veteran. He reached up and placed his thumb against the meaty portion between his opponent's thumb and forefinger and curled his fingers around the pinky, then yanked down while twisting the wrist outward. Tendons popped under the sudden strain, and the man emitted a yelp that Bolan cut short with an uppercut to the point of the jaw. Despite the man's size, the punch had enough power behind it to knock the man into the chintzy crosshatch facade that lined the walls of the vestibule. The wall gave under the man's weight, and he collapsed to the ground amid dust and splintered wood.

Bolan kept his weapons holstered, not wanting to create additional panic on the part of the customers. There were a few in the restaurant with small kids, so Bolan issued a warning that the place was closed and everyone should make themselves scarce. One crew of three men at a table made for weapons concealed in their coats while the rest of the customers headed for the door. The Executioner had no choice but to bring the FNC slung on his shoulder into the act if he didn't want his mission to end right there.

Not a single man even came close to firing as Bolan sprayed the table with a maelstrom of 9 mm slugs, sweeping the muzzle in a corkscrew pattern. Rounds punched through flesh and left gaping holes in their wakes. The men twitched and twittered under the ceaseless staccato of firepower from the autorifle. One of the hoods was nearly decapitated by the flurry of lead poured on them, and the metal storm left a gory mess in the seat and walls of the booth where the quartet had made its stand.

Bolan wasn't sure where to start looking, but as he saw no sign in the dining area of the two men he sought, he figured they were probably in a back room beyond the kitchen. Bolan burst through the pair of swing doors marked as the kitchen by an overhead sign, crouched with the FNC held at the ready. He caught movement in his peripheral vision and turned in time to see a short, Hispanic man yelling and charging him with a massive kitchen knife held at the ready. Bolan got the FNC up in time to block the downward thrust, then twisted the stock of the weapon so the sling entangled the man's hand and wrenched the knife from his opponent's grasp before using the lever to execute a hip toss. The man landed hard on the linoleum with a crunch and a groan.

Bolan turned in time to see the two men he'd observed going into the restaurant as they emerged from a freezer. They both looked at him in complete surprise—apparently they hadn't heard the shooting inside the freezer. Each man carried a small, leather satchel Bolan assumed would be filled with money from the sales. So they were bagmen for Guerra's operation. That was just fine.

The smaller of the two saw the wicked-looking assault

rifle clutched in Bolan's grasp. He dropped his satchel and raised his hands. The second wasn't quite as smart and clawed for hardware in a holster beneath his jacket. Bolan easily acquired the frantic target and quickly squeezed the trigger. The short burst caught the guy full in the abdomen. The impact lifted him from his feet and slammed him into the freezer door. He slid to the ground, leaving a gory wash of blood in his wake that shimmered as it dissipated on the ribbed, stainless-steel door.

Bolan crossed the distance in three steps and relieved the prisoner of his weapon. He backed him up a safe distance and then hauled the body of the man's deceased comrade clear so he could access the freezer. "Open the door," he ordered.

The young gangster stared at him with venom in his eyes but complied. As he did, Bolan opened the satchel he'd dropped and found it stuffed with stacks of bills bound together with paper noting the denominations. He looked through the doorway of the open freezer and had to wait while the initial swirl of fog dissipated before noting the massive walk-in freezer had rows of frozen goods along the two main shelves. Toward the back were some additional compartments. Bolan escorted his prisoner inside with a prod from the FNC in the small of the back. The man knew what Bolan was looking for, and went straight to the compartments and opened them up without being asked. Inside one of them the soldier saw everything from tiny bindles up to full kilo bags of cocaine. Shelves behind another door contained marijuana distributed in quarter, halves and full ounces, plus a couple of multipound bags wrapped in brown butcher paper.

"You guys have been busy," Bolan said. "Stand aside."

The man complied, and Bolan reached into the bag at his side to remove four quarter-pound sticks of C-4 plastique he'd prepared beforehand. He placed them strategically inside each of the compartments and then hustled himself and the man out of there, closing the door behind him. He held up the remote detonator with purpose and tripped the switch. The explosions were muffled, but Bolan could tell his handiwork had done the trick.

He turned to his captive. "You work for Guerra?"

The kid nodded once.

"Where is he?"

"I ain't telling you nothing, *cabrón*," the hood replied.

Bolan nodded for a moment and then grabbed a fistful of the punk's shirt. "Okay, then you can tell *him* something. Tell him I'm coming. Tell him I know he killed Gary Marciano and his wife, and that he ordered that witness murdered. This is only the beginning and before the night's over I'll destroy every scummy operation he's running. You got that?"

The kid nodded quickly and Bolan spun him and sent him running. The gangbanger stumbled once over the body at the entrance to the kitchen but quickly regained his balance and hightailed it out of there. Bolan waited a minute before picking up the satchel and leaving it near the front entrance. He'd let Smalley take credit for seizing the money. Now that he'd shaken things up a bit, Bolan figured it was time to drop the worm into the water.

And the Executioner knew a hood like Mario Guerra would have no trouble taking the bait.

5

In response to Bolan's request, Price and Kurtzman immediately set to work on finding any connections that would link Mario Guerra's Hillbangers operations with the influx of illegal immigrants into the area.

With his customary adeptness, Kurtzman accessed the databases that warehoused information mined from INS computers via an invisible link he'd established with them to Stony Man's massive mainframe systems. First, they evaluated the information regarding the nature of the immigrants and their countries of origin. To no surprise, the highest number was Mexico. But as they dug further they began to see an interesting pattern emerge, one that lent considerable merit to Mack Bolan's theories regarding MS-13 and the immigration problems faced by the entire area.

"Wait! Hold it, Bear," Price said. They were seated in the Computer Room of the Annex, reviewing frames of information scrolling across Kurtzman's monitor.

Kurtzman sat hunkered over the terminal keyboard. He tapped the back paging key and then looked at the screen, squinting to see what it was that had commanded Price's attention.

"What is it?" Kurtzman asked.

"Right there, that table of statistics regarding countries of origin," Price replied. "The INS is required to submit a data analysis report every five years for executive review. That report is dated 2005 and covering years from 2000 to 2004."

"And?"

"Look at the numbers on the grid by year. Prior to 2004, Cuba was number two *consistently* for country of origin. Then there's Russia at third, and El Salvador's way down on the list. Then in 2004 it spiked, jumping way up in ranking to second, bypassing all those other countries." She looked at Kurtzman. "Striker was right, Bear. After the 2003 crackdown, MS-13 changed tactics and decided to flood the area with as many illegal immigrants as possible. They knew it would shift the focus of the government, and cause them to divert resources to combat the problem."

"Okay, but why didn't anyone see this pattern emerging?" Kurtzman said. "It's so blatantly obvious."

Price shrugged and sighed. "Who knows? There's no question that half the oversight committee members in Wonderland don't even read these reports in detail."

"Okay," Kurtzman said, "so how is this going to assist Striker in his particular mission?"

"It might not help much with what he has to do here in the States," Price said. "But it would definitely give him a clue as to potential locations of this secret MS-13 headquarters."

"How so?"

"Well, every single person processed by INS is finger-printed and his immediate ancestry entered into a database. Government regulations require we return any illegal immigrant in our custody to their country of origin in as good or better condition than when they were confined. That means we feed them, give them a clothing allowance and provide a general health exam, primarily to screen them for any potential communicable or social diseases."

"You're thinking that if we extract the data from those records we'll be able to find some kind of pattern, tabulate commonalities and narrow it down to a few select areas of El Salvador."

"Exactly," she said. "Akira's already written the SIFT program that applies algorithms to terrorist actions to find common markers based on countries, motives, attack types and so forth. Any reason the program couldn't be modified to do that work for us?"

"None at all," Kurtzman said. "Although it will take a little time."

"How long?"

"Couple of hours," Kurtzman said.

"Do it," she said. "Meanwhile, I'll let Hal know and once we have the results we'll see about our next move."

"Let Hal know what?" Brognola's voice resounded as he entered the Computer Room.

Price looked at the Stony Man chief and expressed concern. "You look harried, Hal."

"I just got off a *very* long phone conversation with the Man. He's less than ecstatic about the recent fireworks in Herndon."

"He understands the necessity?" Price inquired.

Brognola nodded as he reached into his pocket for a roll of antacids. He kept a supply of them on his person at all times. "Although that doesn't help us much. It seems that Mike Smalley is tugging on the ears of everyone who will listen to him, including a federal judge. I hope Striker comes up with some results soon."

"He will," Price said.

"What have you found out?"

Price told him about their discovery of the illegal immigration and their plans to surf the data for common factors that might point them to the location of the MS-13 headquarters in El Salvador. She also brought him up to speed on Bolan's most recent activities in the south part of Herndon, and noted that plans were set for Bolan's trip to Los Angeles.

"Jack will be leaving for Dulles in a couple of hours," she concluded.

Brognola nodded. "I've managed to convince the AG's office we need to reach out to the NVGTF and ask for their involvement in helping Smalley crack down on the gangs there. The more hoods we can clear off the streets, the less difficult it will make things for Striker when he finally drops the hammer on Guerra."

"Well, he's taken out their numbers rackets and main source of drugs distribution in the city," she said. "And he's sent a *personal* message to Guerra to let him know the hits would keep coming until he'd closed down every operation they oversaw. That's going to have far-reaching effects on Guerra."

"It's also going to get the attention of the L.A. and El Salvador operations, which was exactly the kind of notice Guerra likely wanted to avoid," Brognola concluded.

"You think the MS-13 brass will respond in kind?" Kurtzman asked.

Brognola shook his head. "It's not likely they'll have time. Striker's moving fast on this. He expects to clear things out in Herndon within twenty-four hours, and by my clock he's ahead of schedule. Assuming he finds and eliminates Guerra and the Herndon leadership tonight, he could very well be in L.A. by early morning."

Kurtzman let out a long whistle, and Price said, "There's no way they could retaliate that quickly."

"Right," Brognola said. "The mission in L.A. could take a bit longer, though. Not only are there the sheer numbers to contend with, there are also many more layers to peel back."

"We'll deal with the layers," Price said. "And Striker will take care of the numbers—every last one."

6

San Salvador

Serafin Cristobal listened carefully to the details relayed to him by Mario Guerra with great interest. The news of their failure to successfully hit the surviving members of Marciano's family didn't disturb him nearly as much as the fact that their operations had been disrupted severely by the actions of this lone American government man. Things had been operating smoothly until Guerra convinced Cristobal to approve the hit on the federal prosecutor's family and his key witness. This matter had gotten out of hand and with consequences that were wholly unacceptable.

When Guerra finished his report, Cristobal remained silent for a time. He had learned as the Le Gango Jefe never to speak too quickly to such matters. Every situation presented was unique, and this one was no exception, regardless of how much the situation might concern him. To respond too quickly would make him seem to his underlings as impetuous and unthinking. Waiting too long would leave them with a sense he was weak and indecisive. Particularly to a young, impressionable man like Mario Guerra.

Not that Cristobal didn't have his own spies within the ranks of each cell. This, too, was the secret to great leadership. He prided himself on the intelligence network he'd built within his organization, and how effectively he had utilized its services when times called for it. This seemed to be one of these times, since it had become apparent Guerra's local people couldn't finger this individual who seemed bent on wreaking havoc on their Herndon operations—operations that could eventually lead a trail straight back to his front door.

Cristobal didn't need that kind of problem right now.

"You still have no idea who this man is," he finally said quietly.

"No, *jefe*," Guerra replied.

Cristobal smiled when he heard the slight shake in Guerra's voice. Good, his initial silence had concerned the shot-caller. "Just from what you've told me, Mario, it would seem this man has some sort of personal vendetta against you," he said.

"It does?"

"Of course it does. Why else would he have left one of your men alive to deliver that message to you?"

"But I don't know who he is," Guerra protested. "I don't even know who he works for, *jefe*."

"He seems to know you. Is it possible you had maybe a slip of the tongue while inside the system, Mario? Even a little one? If so, it's perfectly understandable, but you had best confess to me now if you did."

"No! I swear, I said nothing to the cops. I swear on my unborn son's eyes!"

"That may very well be the result if I discover later you have lied to me," Cristobal replied icily. "But you have always shown yourself trustworthy, so for now I will continue to think only good things about you. In the meantime, it seems obvious your people are incapable of dealing with this one man. So I guess I'm compelled to send someone who specializes in this kind of thing to assist you."

"Thank you, *jefe*. What do you wish me to do?"

"Nothing," Cristobal instructed him curtly. "I will make a

call and you will wait by the phone until you hear from this man. You will not send anyone else. You will close down all operations until he comes to you. This man is an expert in such matters. I have used him before with great success."

"I understand, *jefe*. I shall wait for him to contact me."

"You do that, Mario."

Cristobal gently put the receiver in the cradle before uttering a curse under his breath. What a snake. Guerra was such a spineless weasel, like a fangless viper who would have maintained a conciliatory manner even if Cristobal were to come there personally and dig his eyeballs out with a spoon. There were moments when Cristobal couldn't stand such *men*. Not that Guerra really qualified for the title—he lacked the right kind of experience. He'd reached his position through maneuvering and bootlicking the more seasoned shot-callers while serving in Los Angeles. After this situation was dealt with, he would have to see about getting Guerra replaced.

For now, however, he needed to locate the American agent and destroy him once and for all. This could not continue, to be sure.

Cristobal had already alerted his so-called specialist to potential problems. He didn't know the identity of this individual—the man had forbidden ever meeting in person—but he'd handled a few of the previous jobs with professionalism and discretion, *and* with assurances there would be no ties to Cristobal or MS-13. He hadn't failed yet.

Cristobal picked up the phone and dialed the number from memory. He connected to an answering service that advised they would give their client the message. Twenty minutes later, the phone rang.

"You called?" a rich, baritone voice said.

Cristobal had never been quite able to pinpoint the accent. It was European, not German but something close. Maybe

Czech? "The little issue we discussed earlier appears to be spiraling out of control."

"I've heard," the man said. "You are ready for me to take care of it?"

"Yes."

"All right. The usual arrangements, half up front—"

"And the balance on confirmation," he said. "Yes, I know. And one other thing."

"What?"

"Do this quickly. As quickly as possible," Cristobal said.

"Understood."

Cristobal waited for something else but instead heard a click in his ear—the conversation had apparently been terminated. He waited until he heard a dial tone and then replaced the handset. He sat back, picked up his water-cooled pipe and had the skinny woman seated at his feet light the leafy contents of the bowl. He inhaled deeply on the pipe, then closed his eyes and leaned his head back. As he let the smoke out slowly he felt a pair of hands reach to undo the tie of his loose-fitting pants.

And Cristobal smiled at the thought of all the good things in store for him.

CHIEF MIKE SMALLEY headed for the seedy motel in south Herndon immediately after he cleared the scene at the Tres Hermanos restaurant. As he drove, his thoughts turned to what he'd witnessed in just the past eight hours. From MS-13's failed attack on the Marciano funeral to the destruction of the largest drug distribution pipeline in the greater Washington metro area, Cooper had demonstrated his uncanny knack for hitting the gang where it seemed to hurt the most and would do the greatest good for Smalley's jurisdiction.

Thus far, he didn't feel like he had really lived up to their end of the bargain. Taking Mario Guerra's thugs off the streets had proved quite challenging, since the thugs were nowhere to be found. Any other time Smalley would have been grateful for such scarcity, but in this case he could see how critical it was to the success of Cooper's plans. He just couldn't shake the feeling he'd let Cooper down a bit. While Smalley still didn't approve of Cooper's methods on the surface, deep down he admired the hell out of the guy.

Smalley reached the motel and drove around the block several times before pulling his unmarked unit into the lot and driving around back. He found Cooper's Mustang GT parked in a space closest to the nearest exit, nose pointed out. He grinned and shook his head—the guy definitely knew his business. Smalley climbed from his unit, located the room number he'd obtained earlier and rapped lightly on the door. As he waited for Cooper to answer, he looked over the rest of the tiny lot. Empty. Not another single tenant anywhere in sight.

Cooper opened the door and stepped aside to admit the police chief. Smalley crossed the threshold and immediately took note of the Beretta pistol Cooper held at his side in ready position to deal whatever reply might be required at a moment's notice. And holy crap, if the guy wasn't actually dressed in a commando-style suit, just like the witnesses had described. Cooper made for an imposing sight indeed.

Smalley produced a half-grin. "I see you like to be prepared."

Bolan closed the door. As he holstered the pistol he replied, "Always. How did you know where to find me?"

"You kidding?" Smalley said. "I grew up in this town, I know everybody. Wasn't too difficult to figure it out when Teresa at the front desk called me up and told me some big suspicious-looking character just checked into her motel in the middle of the week, and paid cash to boot."

"A hundred dollars doesn't go as far as it used to, I see," Bolan replied.

"Nope."

"What can I do for you?" Bolan said, gesturing toward one of the two chairs at a small table that actually folded into the wall when not in use.

Smalley sat. "I just came from your handiwork at the restaurant."

"You found the money?"

Smalley nodded. "And the note. Thanks."

"Put it to good use."

"I will." Smalley cleared his throat and said, "I just thought I'd stop by to tell you we haven't had much luck rounding up Guerra's goons. I'm a bit surprised, actually. Normally there's no shortage of bad guys here in Herndon."

"It doesn't surprise me at all," the big guy replied. "I think after their little fiasco today at the park that Guerra's planning something big."

"And that is?"

"Some sort of retaliation." Bolan frowned. "Against me."

"Well, you did push the guy's buttons, that's for sure. There's still time to change your mind about getting some extra help from us."

Bolan shook his head. "Thanks, but no thanks. I've got this just about wrapped up. In fact, I'll be clearing out of here in the next four to six hours. Just as soon as I finish what I came here to do."

Smalley could hardly believe his ears. "You're that close?"

"After I hit the restaurant, I sent one of Guerra's bagmen back to him with a message."

"You sure he got it?"

"Loud and clear," Bolan replied with a nod.

"And you think that'll be enough to draw him out?"

He favored Smalley with a cold, hard smile. "No doubt about it."

MARIO GUERRA TRIED to not appear intimidated by the presence that entered his apartment.

He'd never met this man before, but he had clearly been bred for one purpose: killing. The man known as Segador— Spanish for "reaper"—stood head and shoulders above Guerra, maybe six foot four, with light brown hair and piercing slate-blue eyes. He had an accent that Guerra couldn't pinpoint. Not that Guerra had any true concern about the guy—he didn't care where he came from, as long as he could take care of this federal agent.

The other imposing thing about the guy was the strange way he dressed. He wore black combat boots, camouflage fatigue pants and a forest-green turtleneck of stretch material. A long, weathered, black leather trench coat covered his clothes. And in the dim light Guerra caught glimpses of a knife and a garrote on his belt—realizing there were likely other instruments of death buried under the coat.

"His name is Matt Cooper," Segador stated. "His dossier says he is an agent with the U.S. Justice Department, part of a special detachment to Homeland Security. Obviously, that record is forged. It's more probable he works for a covert arm of the government, maybe a military one."

"Look, man, all I know is this guy's become a real pain in the ass and El Jefe says that you're the one to take care of it."

Segador nodded. "I shall."

"You want some of my men to help you?"

"No, they would only be in the way. This man sent your boy back to you with his tail between his legs to convey that message for a very specific reason. I think he had hoped to flush you out. He would, therefore, expect you to send some small force against him."

"He doesn't want that," Guerra replied with bravado, standing more erect to look bigger than he was. "My men would be—"

"Slaughtered like lambs," Segador said cuttingly. "Just as the others were. The only reason you have not succeeded against this man is because you fail to realize you are dealing with a professional soldier. This man is no whelp who will cower at the mere sight of inexperienced toughs. He is well-armed, experienced and dangerous—undoubtedly a veteran of countless such operations as these. He has demonstrated a fearless resolve against overwhelming odds. And I would imagine whoever pulls his strings has ordered him to terminate you."

Guerra became livid. "What did you say?"

"It only makes sense." Segador produced a scoffing laugh. "What else do you think his purpose would be in all of this? The government knows with Marciano and their key witness dead that they cannot prosecute you legitimately, now. This man's very activities going unchecked, then, could only mean someone very high up in government has authorized your summary execution. Perhaps even under presidential order."

"I'll kill them!" Guerra shouted, slamming his fist into his palm. "I'll kill all those *bastardos*."

Pure hardness, like frost-coated steel, dripped in Segador's reply. "You will do nothing of the kind. You will stay out of my way and let me handle this situation."

"You answer to—"

"No one. I am a freelancer compensated by your boss to deal expediently with matters such as these. You had your chance to deal with this individual, and you failed. Now if you wish to save yourself any further embarrassment, I would strongly advise that you do not send any more of your wet-behind-the-ears bangers to their deaths. I would not want to mistake them for the enemy."

"Fine," Guerra conceded. "But tell me this. If we could not beat this Cooper with sheer numbers, what makes you think you can take him out on your own?"

"Because he is not anticipating me," Segador replied. "He is expecting untrained gang members to launch a full-blown assault—not a carefully prepared and unobtrusive ambush by a skilled *expert* in subversive warfare. In other words, I am more like this man than you can ever surmise. I know how he works, how he thinks and how we will react to, shall we say, certain stimuli. And because of that, I become like a natural predator that will ultimately provoke his undoing."

Santa Maria, Guerra thought, but this guy talked like a freaking encyclopedia. Guerra trusted Cristobal implicitly, but he couldn't say he bore the same confidence in this clown. Despite Segador's very valid point that his men had been unable to overcome Cooper, this almost mystical approach to the problem didn't sit very well with Guerra. He would let Segador do whatever he saw fit, but there wasn't any way in hell he'd sit by and do nothing. They needed a backup plan—Guerra always liked to have a backup plan. One that he would lead personally. Many good homeboys had died because they were unprepared for Cooper, but things would be different now that he had some idea of what they were up against. He would call in reinforcements and be ready in case Segador failed.

"If that is what you think," Guerra said, "then I will wait here for you to contact me and let me know it is done."

"You will not hear from me again. When it's done, I will contact your boss and he can give you the news at a time he finds convenient. Good evening."

With that, Segador turned and left Guerra's massive apartment that doubled as his base of operations. He watched as the man let himself out, waited awhile to make sure he was gone and then picked up the phone. A groggy voice finally answered on the fifth ring.

"Yo, Herman, it's me. I need you here in an hour. And bring your boys."

7

Guerra was a fool. A child and a fool who didn't know when to leave things to professionals, Andries Blood thought.

Blood, aka Segador, had been in the assassination business for many years, and he could never understand why powerful and intelligent men like Cristobal insisted on surrounding themselves with idiots. Guerra, barely twenty-two years old, was unfit to lead an expedition of preschoolers through a candy factory, never mind a group of gangbangers with half-baked training in firearms. Blood had spent years perfecting his trade. He'd mastered firearms, explosives and ranked in three martial arts. He'd studied the tactics of great leaders, from Napoleon to Sun Tzu, Washington to Patton, and even those of his own Dutch past: Frederick Henry and Michiel de Ruyter.

Blood, son of a pauper lithographer and his wife, was born and raised in Baarle-Nassau. His iron-deficient blood had prevented his enlistment in any combat-arms-related discipline of the Royal Netherlands Army, although with his high IQ he could have served in transport and logistics. Rather than undergo the humiliation of serving in an unappreciated and uninteresting field of endeavor, Blood took it upon himself to take the meager amassed fortune, the legacy of his parents, to apprentice under private instructors versed in the arts of specialized warfare. He then took freelance assignments to build on his experience until he secured a reputation as a troubleshooter of impeccable abilities.

It was on a recommendation that Blood took that first job with Cristobal so many years ago, and he'd been working for him ever since. Blood couldn't say he enjoyed living in the United States, and he often longed for his home country, but he knew such desires were impractical. Too many people in the Netherlands knew him, if not by reputation then at least by sight, and he couldn't afford that kind of publicity. His business was one of subterfuge, by nature, and he'd spent quite a bit of money and effort to build his ulterior identity, including undergoing plastic surgery—a very risky proposition given his medical condition.

Blood couldn't afford to let someone put all of that at risk because they just wouldn't listen, and that's the problem he knew he had with Guerra. The kid could be his undoing and he wouldn't permit such interference. A call to Cristobal was in order, and Blood made it from a secure sat phone in his car as soon as he left Guerra's apartment—the same apartment in which he'd planted a bug.

"Yes," Cristobal grumbled.

Blood could tell he'd woken the gang leader, not that he really cared. He was in business only to cater to the professional needs of his clients. "I just concluded a meeting with your man."

"And?"

"I do not feel I can count on his cooperation to remain passive until this job is done," Blood replied. "You do understand I deem that a considerable risk to your operation *and* our contract. It cannot be permitted."

"What do you recommend I do about it?"

"What do I always recommend?"

Silence greeted that, and Blood could immediately tell Cristobal was mulling it over. It was not often Blood asked for permission to terminate an employee of a client, but this was a particularly difficult situation, and he did not feel like getting caught off guard because of the petulance and impatience of others who did not know when to listen to those who knew best.

"You're saying there's no other way?"

"No. I am saying that there *may* be no other way. I do not want to fail this job, because I know it is of great importance to your overall success, so you can understand that I will seek you out if I feel the parameters have changed and it may warrant your permission to do what I must if it will see complete success of the original objective."

Cristobal sighed. He stayed silent a moment longer and then said, "I want the original job done, that's what I'm paying you for. Do whatever you feel you have to in order to make that happen."

"Thank you. It shall be as you say."

With that, Blood ended the call, turned his vehicle and headed back to Guerra's apartment. He smiled.

Yes, this night would prove to be most interesting.

THE FINAL BATTLE for control over Herndon began just after the big clock in the downtown historical district struck two in the morning.

When Herman Franco arrived at Guerra's apartment to find the body of his murdered half brother, he experienced a rage like no other. He'd heard the desperation in Guerra's voice, but he'd just figured the guy was overreacting again. He had a tendency to get like that when things got really hot, and that's when Franco would have to come in and settle him down. They might smoke a bowl or two, drink some beers and invite a couple of girls over to take their minds off their worries.

Franco had stepped out of MS-13 to form his own posse, and because he had enough supporters and the new MS-13 shot-caller was blood, nobody messed with them. They had a decent chunk of the territory, and there was only the occasional skirmish between the lower ranking soldiers who knew nothing of the relationship the two gang leaders shared. It wasn't anything personal—they both knew and accepted this was just their business. And each was careful to respect what the other had and not tromp on it. The lines had been clearly drawn, sure, but *this* time someone had stepped over the line.

Franco made a closer inspection of his half brother's body. It looked like he had been shot twice in the back of the head. From the position of Guerra's body, Franco assumed he'd either been on his knees when it happened or he hadn't been looking in the direction of the shooter: that would make it an execution either way. Franco knew there could only be one man responsible, the *federale* who had been running around the town shooting up every MS-13 operation in sight.

"I want the motherfucker who did this," Franco told his crew. "You understand, homeboys? I want this shit."

8

Across town, another entity sat watching a known MS-13 hangout in the barrio of south Herndon.

Bolan had waited for Guerra to show up with his posse at the hotel, but the hit never came—the warrior had to admit this surprised him a bit. He had figured once the message got out, MS-13 would thirst for blood and Bolan would get the job done in Herndon with minimal effort. Once he'd terminated the leadership, Smalley's people would come in and sweep up the pieces. Instead, he'd sat idle at the motel waiting for an attack that never came and had wasted precious hours doing it.

Apparently, Guerra wasn't taking his message very seriously, so Bolan felt the time had come to hit another target and see what he could shake loose. Smalley had managed to glean a piece of intel about a location in the barrio, a clubhouse and party central of sorts, where several of Guerra's people were known to congregate. Included among them was his second in command, a hood named Louie Maragos who, according to Smalley, "Must absolutely be the pride of his family."

Maragos had been implicated in extortion, racketeering, gunrunning and murder, but with the lack of evidence and witnesses to hold Guerra, law-enforcement officials no longer had the goods on any of Guerra's associates either. That included Maragos. Well, that was fine with Bolan. If he couldn't get Guerra's people to take the bait and come to him, he would just have to go to them and restate his message in a way that would leave no misunderstanding about his intentions.

Bolan studied the front of a dark-paneled single story. It occupied a large lot, and a six-foot high chain-link fence encircled the perimeter. As the Executioner swept the grounds with a pair of NVD binoculars, the green haze of the viewer intensified whenever he passed an external light source. He didn't notice any electronic security of any kind, and he hadn't spotted a single sentry. Not surprising—it was a party house, after all, not a secure government facility. The Executioner had to wonder if he hadn't given Guerra the credit he deserved and he was actually walking into a trap here. Bolan lowered the field glasses and considered his options. There were a number of ways to hit a place like this and achieve positive results.

Bolan gave it a little more thought and then decided the best course of action based on the fact that he didn't have any idea how many might be inside, or if he risked hitting innocent targets.

The Executioner climbed from his vehicle, still in full combat gear, and removed the M-16 A-2/M-203 from the trunk of the Mustang GT. He'd already cleaned and resupplied his small arms with fresh ammunition in preparation for the MS-13 retaliation. Bolan now removed a half-dozen high explosive 40 mm grenades and placed them in the various concealed pockets of his blacksuit. He loaded one into the breech of the grenade launcher, slammed it home and then closed his trunk and took up a position behind a light post that provided an effective field of fire over the entire property.

Bolan adjusted the range finder sight, settled on the first in line of a half dozen or so cars parked along the street in front of the building and squeezed the trigger. The buttstock kicked against his shoulder with the force of a 12-gauge shotgun and a pop-plunk report. The 40 mm HE grenade struck the back window of a beat-up Chevy and exploded. A bright, red-orange fireball immediately engulfed the interior and the bluish white gases expended enough energy to blow out all the windows. The gasoline tank had to have caught just right because a secondary explosion followed a moment later. The Executioner had already shifted his attention to the next car in line. He delivered another 40 mm grenade to that vehicle with similar effects. He'd just lit up number four when the MS-13 crew burst from the front door of the house, weapons in hand.

Bolan nodded with satisfaction as he aligned his sights on vehicle number five and triggered the M-203. Glass and metal shards whistled through the air, and the flaming wreckage from all the vehicles lit up the night like a mob carrying torches. The flames and heat were so intense the gangbangers couldn't get too close without risking burns to their skin or choking on the thick, black smoke that roiled from the vehicles. Bolan didn't hesitate to take immediate advantage of the heat, noise and confusion.

The warrior locked the butt of the M-16 A-2 against his shoulder, pressed his cheek to the stock and centered on the first target. He thumbed the selector to single-round mode and squeezed the trigger. The first 5.56 mm NATO round traveled the distance at a velocity of about 850 meters per second and struck the target in the side of the neck. Blood from the carotid artery spurted visibly as the bullet fragmented and tore through cartilage of the esophagus and windpipe before finally lodging in the neck muscles.

Bolan turned the muzzle slightly until his sights found the second target—a pair of hoods caught off guard by the sudden demise of their comrade—and triggered two more rounds. The first hood caught the round in his midsection, while the second round took the other target in the chest, exploding his heart on impact with enough force to knock him off his feet.

Bolan broke cover and raced across the street to take up a different position, concerned he'd used that one as long as he could without risking them pinpointing his location. Even though the frantic mass and chaos of the moment had obviously caught them unawares, an assuming soldier could wind up a dead soldier. Bolan found a new position behind a vehicle and raised the M-16 A-2 to his shoulder once more. As he looked for his next target, a trio of young women emerged from the house. They looked to be hardly more than teenagers, and one of them cradled a bundle in her arms. Those weren't groceries she carried.

As the young woman ran past one of the gangbangers, he grabbed her arm and began to yell something at her in Spanish. She and her two girlfriends started yelling back at him, and tried to break free, but the kid wasn't buying. One of the young women flanked him and jumped onto his back. She started beating him on top of the shoulders and head, and Bolan didn't have to speak Spanish fluently to recognize some of vernacular she used. The kid finally tossed her off and she landed hard on the dried, frozen grass of the front yard. He then turned on her and raised a pistol to shoot her.

Bolan reacted.

The warrior snap-aimed as he thumbed the selector to 3-round bursts and squeezed the trigger. The rounds left the chamber and hit their target dead-on, two catching him in the shoulder and the other splitting his head open. The young women squealed in horror as the banger's lifeless body slumped to the ground—but they were safe. Bolan watched with mild interest as they collected themselves quickly and got the hell out of there.

As the females headed down the street at a good clip, the

remaining half-dozen gangbangers retreated inside the house, apparently convinced they were outmatched by an enemy superior in numbers and firepower. Bolan heard the shrill call of distant sirens and figured he had maybe a minute or two to finish the job here. He broke cover and sprinted down the sidewalk. When he reached the fence, he slung the M-16 A-2 and scaled it easily until he could vault over the top. He landed catlike on the other side and charged the front door as he unleathered his Beretta. The flimsy door gave way under Bolan's kick and practically splintered off its hinges.

The Executioner moved inside and caught several of the hoods just as they had started to swing their weapons in his direction, but Bolan dispatched them easily with single shots aimed center mass. The first two caught 9 mm Parabellum bullets in the chest, and a third round punched through the skull of the last goon at the point of his upper lip. Bolan was on the move again before the bodies of the three gangbangers finished hitting the floor. He reconnoitered the house but didn't encounter any further resistance. The others had to have escaped out the back door. Bolan snapped an AN-M14 TH3 grenade from his LBE harness, yanked the pin and tossed the bomb casually onto the bed in one main room of the house. He delivered identical packages to a love seat in one living area and a couch in another that looked like it had seen plenty of use for a myriad of purposes. Bolan had detected the residual odors of hash, crack and alcohol. Who knew what all had transpired here? It would only serve the best interests of the neighborhood to incinerate the place, and it was far enough from the other homes not to pose a danger.

Bolan had completed his task and left the house just as the thermate-filled grenades began to explode. The Executioner tossed the over-and-under M-16 combo in the backseat, climbed behind the wheel and made the corner at the far end of the street just as police squads turned onto the road at the other end.

Bolan drove a couple of blocks before becoming suspicious of a pair of headlights that had first come into view after he'd turned the corner. It was a strange time of night for a vehicle to be traveling in this part of town, and it seemed more than coincidental that it just happened to be present at the same time as he departed from the neighborhood. Bolan considered evasion but opted against it, realizing this might be the opportunity for which he'd waited. There was no reason for Smalley to tail him, or assign someone to follow him, which left only the enemy as a possibility.

The Executioner slowed enough so that the follower could keep up but not so much as to raise suspicions, alerting his tail that Bolan knew someone was on to him. As he left the barrio, he considered his next move. He needed to get to a location that afforded some running room but was not so populated as to risk endangering civilians. The most probable course would be the Dulles Toll Road—it would be relatively deserted of commuters at this time of morning.

The Executioner recalled seeing some exits on a map that led to a massive industrial park and after several minutes at highway speeds he came upon one of them. Most of the businesses in the park would be closed, and it would provide him enough open ground to stage a welcoming committee. Bolan blew the intersection light at the bottom of the exit ramp and made a hard left that took him beneath the overpass. Here he accelerated, smoothly shifting gears and gaining speed so he could widen the gap enough to buy him planning time.

Bolan reached the unmanned entrance to the industrial park and checked his rearview mirror in time to see the headlights swing into view. He proceeded into the park and took a circuitous road bordering the various lots of the factories and office buildings peppering the complex. The road and pursuit vehicle disappeared from view and Bolan proceeded another hundred yards or so before swinging into an abandoned lot and killing his lights. He maneuvered his vehicle between two smaller buildings adjoining a large warehouse, switched off the engine, slapped the stick into Neutral and coasted to a stop.

Bolan applied the parking brake, snatched the M-16 A-2/ M-203 off the backseat and went EVA.

As he made a beeline for a nearby row of manicured hedges, the headlights of the tail vehicle came into view and then winked out when they drew nearer. That only solidified the theory someone *was* following him. The blackout wouldn't help the driver one bit, but the light from overhead streetlights still illuminated the car adequately enough for Bolan to draw a bead. The Executioner put the weapon butt to his shoulder, aligned the fixed sights on the vehicle and traversed its path with a slight lead. He waited until the vehicle had just passed the point where it came parallel with his position, locked on the tires and squeezed the trigger. With the weapon still in burst mode, three rounds rocketed from the muzzle and struck a front tire.

The vehicle hadn't been traveling that fast, so the driver managed to keep it in control. He ground to a halt, his steering nearly useless under the tire-shredding effects of Bolan's marksmanship. A lone occupant emerged from the driver's side and took cover behind the vehicle. Bolan marked the response as calculated—coupled with the fact that the driver didn't immediately respond by blasting the area with a hail of lead cleared any misgivings the Executioner might have had about his tail. He was dealing with a professional all the way.

Like a patient hunter, the Executioner awaited his prey to give away its exact position. He considered triggering another salvo but decided to wait. His opponent likely didn't have a fix on his location, and he saw no point in doing something to give away the advantage afforded him by concealment.

Bolan waited, content to sit it out as long as needed. The minutes ticked by as he stayed patient and motionless, crouched behind the hedge, ignoring the cramping sensation that crept into his thighs and calves.

Bolan finally detected the bare hint of movement from behind his enemy's vehicle, watched with interest as the target moved into the tall, dry grass behind the road and tried to circumvent his position in a flanking maneuver. Bolan remained patient and confident, certain the right time to engage would present itself. Eventually, he got his chance as a patch of brush rustled about twenty yards up range from the disabled car and a figure emerged at the bend in the access road.

Bolan could see the shadowy form as it bolted across the street and headed for cover behind a small outbuilding. He estimated no more than ten seconds to acquire his target and take it out.

But before he got the chance, the screech of tires distracted him. A pair of dark vehicles rounded the corner of the industrial park entrance and raced up the road, both swerving violently as the drivers tried to maintain some semblance of control. Bolan watched as they drove up to the car that had been tailing him and skidded to a halt. At least a half-dozen armed occupants spilled from the vehicles. In the streetlights he didn't see any colors or symbols identifying them as members of MS-13, but something in their movements told Bolan they were bangers all the same. In the next moment, they opened on the sedan with a furious barrage of autofire that transformed it into scrap metal.

The Executioner returned his attention to where he'd spotted his tail.

The lone figure was gone!

9

"I'm coming out now," announced an instantly recognizable voice over the din of shooting. "I'd appreciate it if you didn't blow my head off."

"You're clear, Smalley," Bolan replied.

The police chief stepped from the shadows of a nearby building and joined the Executioner at the hedge. Bolan had to admit he was surprised to discover it was Smalley who had tailed him here. He couldn't guess why the cop would be so furtive, but he assumed the army of gangbangers now shooting up his car might have something to do with it. After Smalley had dangled the carrot about the party house, he had to have decided to show up and observe Bolan's handiwork— that meant the gang had someone tailing the chief.

"Looks like you were right," Smalley observed.

"About what?"

He nodded toward the gang members as they loaded fresh clips and riddled his car with another hot salvo of lead. "That MS-13 would come calling."

"I don't think they're MS-13."

"They're not, actually, you're right," Smalley replied. "They're part of a gang led by Herman Franco. He's a former member of MS-13 and an ally to Mario Guerra. My inside people think the two may be related somehow, but we're not positive."

"Why would they be after you?"

"I don't know," Smalley replied. "But after you took that shot at me, I radioed for help. We'll have a dozen units here in a few minutes, including a crew from the gang task force."

"You pulled some strings?"

"No," Smalley said with a wry grin. He looked Bolan in the eye and added, "But I think *you* did. They just showed up at the station and offered to help."

"I won't risk putting your people in the line of fire here," Bolan said.

"I don't see how we can avoid it now."

Bolan reached into the satchel at his hip and removed a 40 mm shell. "I do."

The Executioner loaded the shell, took aim and squeezed the trigger of the M-203. The grenade arced perfectly and landed smack dab in the center of the bangers. A brilliant explosion lit the night and carved gashes in the pavement as the heat and shock wave tore limbs from bodies and scattered the men in every direction. The few who had escaped were taken completely off guard by the assault, and Bolan used that confusion to pick off the survivors with deadly accuracy.

Bolan loaded a second shell and aimed for their vehicles, but Smalley restrained his arm.

"Wait," the chief said. "Don't destroy those cars. They may contain some decent intelligence we can use."

Bolan considered the request for a moment and then shrugged and lowered the over-and-under combo. He couldn't see any reason not to grant the cop's request. At this point it was really the chief's show. Bolan had put enough of a dent in the MS-13 operations that they would now be scattered. His only remaining task would be to eliminate Mario Guerra, and he knew that wouldn't prove difficult as long as the shot-caller had remained in Herndon. There was an outside chance that the guy had run, but Bolan had good reasons to doubt it.

Weasels like Guerra would hide but they wouldn't run—it would make him look bad in the eyes of the gang.

As the pair rose and observed the dissipation of flames left in the wake of the grenade, Smalley's cell phone rang. He whipped it off his belt and flipped it open with a flick of his wrist.

"Yeah?" A pause as he listened, then, "You're absolutely sure?" After another minute or so he muttered an affirmation and disconnected the call. He looked at Bolan as he returned the phone to his belt. "That was the patrol sergeant. One of our units just got called for a disturbance at a tenement on the east side. They found Guerra's body."

The Executioner's eyebrows rose in response.

Smalley continued, "It's confirmed. The identity has been double-checked. Somebody executed him. I don't suppose you know anything about that?"

Bolan shook his head. "It wasn't me, Chief. I didn't even know where Guerra was hiding."

"Yeah, well, it looks like someone got to him before you did then." Smalley looked at the decimated gang spread before them and added, "Maybe them?"

"Possibly. But they would have needed a motive. My guess would be whoever's calling the shots on high decided he'd become a liability. Most of their major moneymaking operations here have been obliterated. You can be sure that won't sit well with the big boss."

"What big boss? What the hell are you talking about?"

"After you told me about your influx of illegals, I suspected that someone might be flooding the area to capacity to task out your resources so MS-13 could get on with business as usual. From the intelligence my people have gathered so far, it's looking more like my theory holds water."

"Let me get this straight," Smalley interjected. "You're saying all of this immigration is the doing of MS-13?"

Bolan nodded. "It's a good bet. This goes a lot deeper than you think, Chief. Maybe at one time MS-13 was small gangs here and there, but recently we've seen an epidemic. The deaths of the Marcianos and his key witness prove that much. But this time they acted too quickly, and as a result MS-13 blew its own game wide open. Now it's our turn to give back what all of you have been taking."

Smalley ran a hand through his thinning hair. "Cripes, why the hell didn't I see that? It was so simple."

"It wasn't obvious," Bolan said. "Don't blame yourself, just make sure you don't let up until you've put them down and kept them down. I've hurt them badly here, more than you might suspect. Now I'm passing the torch and it's up to you to finish it."

Smalley nodded and extended his hand. "It seems maybe I misjudged you, Cooper. I could use about a dozen just like you on my force. If you ever need a job…"

There was no need for him to go on and they both knew it. Bolan didn't admit it, but he realized he'd misjudged Smalley in like ways. The guy may have been a hard-ass when it came to following the rules, but that was merely a testament of his dedication to duty. Bolan had his own rules, and he wasn't flexible about them, either—he could hardly blame Chief Mike Smalley for being the same way.

Sirens brought them back from the silent exchange of respect.

"We're playing your song," Smalley said with a grin.

"That's my cue," Bolan said.

"This road has a back access out of here," Smalley replied. "A dirt road, but it should get you clear of the area."

"Thanks," Bolan said.

"Where you headed next?"

"It's probably better you don't know."

As the Executioner turned to leave, Smalley called, "Hey,

Cooper! If it's any consolation, you were already gone by the time I got here. That's my story and I'm sticking to it."

"That'll keep things simpler."

"I'm sure. Good luck, trooper." And as Bolan moved out of ear shot, Smalley added, "And Godspeed."

THE EXECUTIONER didn't have any trouble getting past the widening dragnet Smalley had working to blitz MS-13 activities in every corner of his city. Bolan could only assume the police chief had given him that tip by design. The dirt road led to a hardball which, in turn, ran a back-door route straight to Dulles International Airport. Bolan secured his vehicle in long-term parking where he knew Stony Man's contacts would pick it up. He left all of the weapons behind, then found a place to change into jeans, flannel shirt and a black leather jacket and sneakers. He made his way through the airport and security, eventually winding up at the waiting Gulfstream C-21A, one of several aircraft assigned exclusively for Stony Man operations.

The man who sat in the main cabin with a cup of coffee and a flight chart had proved as versatile as the varied aircraft he flew. Jack Grimaldi looked at Bolan with a broad grin as the Executioner climbed into the aircraft. Grimaldi put his cup and map down on the fold-down table, sat back in the bucket seat of the modified plane and folded his arms.

"Well, aren't you a sight for sore eyes," he quipped.

"Likewise," Bolan said.

The two men shook hands warmly as Grimaldi added, "Damn good to see you, Sarge!"

"You, too. We ready to go?"

"I'm always ready," he said with a contrasting twinkle in his dark eyes.

"Uh-huh," Bolan deadpanned.

"Give me five for preflight and another ten for clearance." Grimaldi looked at his watch and said, "We should be airborne by 0330 hours."

Bolan nodded and dropped into a seat as Grimaldi waved toward the coffeepot, indicating it was fresh before heading to the cockpit. Maybe he'd partake later, but right now the warrior figured the flight across the country would provide a brief respite and a chance at some shut-eye.

It would also give him an opportunity to consider the news of Guerra's death. Smalley had said Guerra was shot execution style, which meant two things: somebody wanted Guerra dead and had hired a professional to do it. Bolan couldn't see any motive for the other gang to kill Guerra, particularly if its leader *had* been related to him. That meant an outside party, likely someone hired by the head of the organization. It was an old story, really. The Mafia had operated in a very similar fashion at one time, and still did in certain circles. When a higher-up started screwing up operations, exposing a head boss or two with liabilities, that generally spelled trouble. Not that Bolan could complain about it; the more infighting they did the better. It was a tactic he had employed many times before, manipulating one criminal society or another until it imploded. They were like rabid dogs, and once they had crossed over the line from allegiance to insanity, they would turn on any perceived threat, whether it was their own blood or not.

It wasn't that Guerra's own people had probably killed him that surprised Bolan; it was how fast they came to making such a decision. Maybe somebody else was up for the title and the top dog in MS-13 had a favored candidate to replace Guerra. Maybe in Bolan's activities he'd simply hit closer to home than he thought. Whatever the case might be, the fact they had assassinated one of their own demonstrated only how desperate they were becoming. That was the effect Bolan wanted to have, which meant his plan was working either way. The purpose was to knock out the leadership, and if MS-13 wanted to help him by offing its own, then he wasn't about to complain.

This did introduce a new complication, however. If MS-13 did hire a contractor to do Guerra, then that meant Bolan would have a new threat to watch for over his shoulder, especially if that contractor followed him to Los Angeles. But Bolan would cross that bridge when he got to it. For now, Guerra had been eliminated and MS-13 operations in Herndon were crumbling, not to mention the head boss was now involved and playing cards out of a dwindling deck. Bolan knew if he pressed the issue, the leader would eventually show his hand.

And when the enemy's cards were showing and the Grim Reaper called all-in, Bolan would play for the pot.

10

El Salvador

In his past life his friends had called him Iggy. To the United States government, particularly Gary Marciano, he was known by the code name Tigre Garra, aka Tiger Claw.

As he pondered his current situation, Ignacio Paz didn't think he reflected either of those identities. At present, he felt more like Trapped Little Rat. His mother was back in the U.S. and suffering from a debilitating illness, his wife was threatening the BATF desk to take the kids and leave, and he was stuck in a foreign country, utterly cut off from further resources, and rapidly running out of cash.

Money had been the one thing that kept Paz out of trouble up to this point, and that kept him in the know about MS-13 activities here in this shit-house of a motel on the outskirts of San Salvador. Money was what he paid the motel owner to keep his mouth shut, money was what he paid the proprietor of the cantina down the block to feed him information, money was what allowed him to afford the whores and the liquor and build his cover as a murderer and drug dealer on the run.

Building a reputation as a scumbag in this dung pile they called a country hadn't proven remotely difficult for Paz. Getting access to the inner workings of MS-13 proved to be another thing entirely. Marciano had missed the last two contacts, and Paz heard ruminations about a major victory in Herndon, one having to do with a contract put out by Serafin Cristobal.

That was one juicy tidbit Paz had managed to squeeze out of the underworld here, proving once more that a harlot could be the undoing of a loquacious drunk. Wine, women and song—that deadly trio had been the undoing of more men than any other in the history of humankind, and knowing that had allowed Paz to exploit just one of the few weaknesses in the closed ranks of MS-13.

Cristobal.

The very name conjured fear in anyone who spoke it and closed the eyes, ears and mouths of the rest whenever they heard it uttered. Unfortunately, the substance of what Paz knew about the guy in liquid terms wouldn't have filled a thimble. Now Paz was running out of time and money, he'd lost contact with the Attorney General's office, and just to put the icing on the cake he now found himself in a stinking, steamy cantina with the gaping maw of a .45-caliber pistol held inches from his face for reasons not yet clear to him.

Fortunately for Paz, the guy standing behind that pistol was red-faced with booze and he seemed pretty unsteady. Not that it took a whole lot of balance to pull a trigger. Still, the fact this Salvadoran was liquored up and Paz had nursed only two beers all night did put the odds in his favor as long as he acted judiciously and with foresight. In his best Spanish and with just the right accent, he tried to reason with the guy.

"Hey, my friend, what's the problem?"

The guy mumbled something, mostly unintelligible, and then went into a fit of coughing that ultimately hocked up a huge chunk of phlegm. The burly, native gunman turned his head and launched the disgusting secretion across the room. Thankfully he hadn't spit on Paz. He'd also turned his attention from the BATF agent, and Paz seized the opportunity. He sidestepped the pistol and got parallel with his opponent before bringing his fist down at a point just behind the butt of the gun while simultaneously bringing his other one up under the man's elbow right at the point of the funny bone. This redirected the muzzle toward the floor while jarring the ulnar nerve at the elbow, knocking the pistol from the man's grasp. The gun hit the ground without going off, but Paz was too busy neutralizing the threat to notice. He delivered an elbow to the guy's ribs, followed by a knee to the groin and then punched him in the side of the head with every bit of force he could muster.

The guy's head rocked to the side as he collapsed into the bar—the liquor did the rest. His body folded like an accordion, and he landed on the dusty, grimy floor with a thud.

Winded, Paz reached down and scooped the pistol off the floor. He dropped the magazine and jacked the slide, peeved to find the guy didn't even have a round chambered, and then tossed the pistol across the room with a disgusted wheeze. Paz looked at the few patrons left in the cantina, started to walk out and then thought better of it and tossed a few coins at the proprietor before walking out. Hush money.

Paz stuck his hands in his pockets as he sauntered down the broken, splintered wooden walkway of the storefronts in the direction of that rat hole called a motel. Hell, he'd been in American slum tenements nicer than that. Still, he had a job to do and he planned to do it no matter what kind of trouble it brought him. He'd come too far to give up now, he didn't give a shit what his supervisors back in Washington said or how many lawyers his wife threatened them with.

Let it go, he thought.

Paz considered his options. Marciano had provided a way out for him, a sort of panic phrase if things got hot enough and he needed to make a quick exit, but it hardly did him any good if he didn't have anybody to use it with. Given Marciano had missed the last two check-ins, Paz could only assume something had gone horribly wrong and he'd been left high and dry. Well, he wasn't going to let that scare him. He hadn't left his country and family and come down here for nothing. He'd get the goods on Cristobal soon enough, and when he did he'd act on the information whether Marciano told him to go or not.

For now, he needed to keep his head down and his ears open; something would break soon enough. Serafin Cristobal and MS-13 were going down.

One way or another.

11

A soft, steady beep pulled Bolan from sleep. Instantly alert, he looked up to see a small, red LED on a nearby console flashing in sync with the beeping. It was Stony Man calling.

Bolan hit the stub to turn on the Web cam and engage the audio-visual linkup to the Farm's secure communications satellite. The screen pixilated from darkness into displaying Barbara Price's face.

Price smiled. "Sorry to wake you."

"Just recharging the batteries. Based on the time, Jack would have been waking me up in a little while anyway."

"Yes, we're tracking the plane and Bear said you're about twenty minutes out."

"What's the buzz?" Bolan asked.

"We finished tracking the source of the immigration problem," she replied, "and we're convinced the operations are headquartered in San Salvador. We don't have an exact location, but we did manage to pinpoint some rather suspicious activities within the country that lead us to believe MS-13 is in full swing down there."

A picture of a stout-faced Hispanic with long brown hair and heavily lidded eyes materialized on the dual LCD panel positioned alongside the one with the Web cam. Bolan immediately began to search his mental files but drew a blank.

"Recognize this guy?"

Bolan shook his head.

"His name is Serafin Cristobal. He's wanted by law-enforcement agencies across the greater Americas as well as Interpol on at least a dozen charges. International racketeering, murder-for-hire, gunrunning, drug smuggling, sex slavery trade…you name it, Cristobal's into it. Just the sort of guy who could oversee a gang like MS-13."

"My feeling exactly," Bolan interjected. "Any known associates?"

"Well, we have a source who's been busy cross-cataloging a database of local terror groups and gangs with known criminals operating outside the U.S. He and Kurtzman went to work scanning LAPD police intake blotters and crime reports that matched known methods employed by Cristobal, specifically gang-centric. We got a ton of hits on an MS-13 cell in East L.A. led by a shot-caller named Charles Camano, aka Chico."

"And you think he can lead us to Cristobal."

"Almost certainly," Price replied without hesitation. "Camano's reputation is well-known inside both MS-13 and the law-enforcement community all up and down the West Coast. He has ties into La Eme, the Spanish Mafia and the Central American drug syndicate. He was also one of several shot-callers arrested in the nationwide raid architected by Gary Marciano based on the statements given by Ysidro Perez, not to mention he's been implicated in several major sex-slavery rings."

"Any intelligence on operational locations?"

"I knew you'd ask," she said with a wink. "And, in fact, we decided to look ahead to that. There's a section in East L.A. affectionately known as Amor Línea, Spanish for Love Row."

"Cute."

"That's what I said. Anyway, every prostitute and pimp who operates in that neighborhood works for Camano. Nobody does any kind of business in that area, sex, drugs or otherwise, without his blessing. He also runs a major business in the area, allegedly a nonprofit, which Marciano's files note is suspect as a front for his escort services."

"Is that what they call it?" Bolan quipped with a shake of his head.

Price sighed and replied, "The oldest profession in the world is still a profitable one. This guy does anything, Striker. Bondage, pornography, snuff films, groupie parties, the works."

"I get the picture," Bolan said. "Sounds like as good a place as any. Maybe he's not the only link to Cristobal, but he's the most solid one. Plus, it wouldn't hurt to put him out of business."

Price nodded. "I wish we had more to give you, but that's the best we've been able to come up with. Even with our resources, it would seem Mr. Camano has managed to cover his master's tracks quite well."

The Executioner's cold blue eyes flashed. "Not for long."

RATHER THAN LAND at LAX, Grimaldi had decided to set down in a small, private county airport on the fringes and proceed to a hangar maintained by Stony Man.

"We'll avoid any uncomfortable security checks, and it will allow us to split without hassle."

Bolan nodded. He'd already stripped, cleaned up with a dry soap compound and redressed in his civilian clothes. The Executioner knew from Price's description he wouldn't have the luxury of moving into Love Row in full combat gear. To arrange such an operation would require soliciting the cooperation of too many agencies, and Bolan knew they didn't have that kind of time. No, this operation would require a measurable degree of subtlety and gathering of intelligence through a soft probe before he could make a hit. The numbers were running down, especially for Ignacio Paz. Bolan had no way of knowing if Paz was even still alive, but he had to make the assumption Marciano would have hired a guy resourceful enough to fly under the radar for some time, perhaps even indefinitely.

Stony Man had managed to procure one lead from Paz's wife, a young and vivacious woman with three kids who didn't have the slightest qualms about raising the roof with Paz's superiors. Unfortunately, while Bolan could empathize with her, he realized the BATF would be at a complete loss since Paz's loan out to Marciano wouldn't have necessarily called for Paz's higher-ups to be privy to the nature of such sensitive operations. Marciano's detailed records did indicate there was a code Paz could use to indicate distress, but without a known mechanism for contacting him, it remained a moot point. Brognola had managed to use his influence with Justice to get the BATF and DEA to reach out to their contacts in El Salvador to see if they could get a line on Paz's whereabouts, but it wasn't looking good.

As things stood, Paz's very life rested in the hands of the Executioner.

Bolan didn't think too much of having one more life added to his conscience—particularly not the life of a federal cop—but he didn't get to pick and choose these missions. They chose him, and Fate was a master with one hellacious and warped sense of humor. The Executioner had brought his war this far, and he knew there would be any turning back now.

AS THE SUN CLIMBED toward late morning in downtown Los Angeles, Bolan drove his rental vehicle into East L.A. and parked it within a mile of Love Row. Rush hour automobile and pedestrian traffic clamored along the streets and sidewalks as business commuters competed with other bikes, motor scooters, transit buses and one another to get where they were going. Bolan figured his vehicle would be safer here while he reconnoitered Love Row on foot. He walked a few blocks and then used an alley to cut out of the business district and head into the red-light one.

Outside, the echo of honking horns and the sounds of rush hour echoed faintly in the already hot, stiff air. It seemed to Bolan as if he'd simply stepped out of time and place into another world entirely. The streets were all but completely deserted, the storefronts of clubs, smoke shops and other sordid businesses all barred with retractable grates. A warm wind blew off the ocean and wound its way through the labyrinth of concrete and steel, hustling garbage and paper down the street. Bolan caught movement out of the corner of his eye and reached for the Beretta beneath the navy blue windbreaker he'd traded for his leather jacket, but it was only a couple of alley cats who knocked over some trash and bottles from an overstuffed wastebasket.

Bolan felt exposed standing there in the open, as if he were the last man alive, but he knew there were others secured behind those locked and barred doors. This would be the time for him to get information and ask questions, a time when Chico's prostitutes and pimps would be least prepared for him. Nighttime was when things got fired up in a place like this, and although Bolan could be a creature of the night, he preferred to think like a soldier. The soundest military tactic he knew was to exploit the enemy at dawn, and this time of morning for the denizens of a place like Love Row would have the same effect.

Bolan proceeded down the sidewalk with confidence in his gait. His eyes scanned the area ahead, looking for any sort of threat. At one point, he stopped to look down a dead-end alley. Two homeless people, a male and female, were restlessly picking through crates and trash boxes thrown out back the night before in hopes of procuring a treasure or two, something that would bring them enough coin for food or, in a more realistic scenario, liquor.

Bolan continued past the alley until he reached a flight of steps that led up to a stoop recessed in the row of businesses. A dead neon sign above the door advertised City of Angels Inn, Cheap Rooms. Bolan tugged on the door, propped open just slightly by a rock, and stepped into the vestibule. Cracked, checkerboard linoleum lined the floor and despite the door being open, it was stifling hot inside, almost as if the entryway and foyer beyond doubled as a boiler room. Mailbox units lined one wall—an oddity for a hotel where supposedly the stay was temporary—although they appeared dusty with disuse and only one sported a name: Jones, L. in Room 10.

Bolan studied his surroundings for a minute and then proceeded deeper into the motel. He followed a narrow hallway that bordered the staircase just off the foyer, which eventually opened onto a wide room containing a desk, a door marked as a restroom and a counter. Nobody occupied the office, and looking at the disuse and dust Bolan had to wonder how long it had been since someone had manned the place. The Executioner turned on his heel, headed back to the stairs and began to climb. When he reached the first-floor landing, he withdrew the Beretta. He listened for any sound of life, anything that might indicate someone waiting for him, but he didn't hear a thing. He followed the hallway to the end and selected the first door. The only way he would get information was by conducting a room to room search.

Bolan reached for the door handle, careful to keep his body to one side, but the sound of a door opening at the far end commanded his attention. He froze, pistol held casually at his side, and watched as a woman with frazzled blond hair, wearing cyan hot pants and a black tube top stepped into view. She made a point of closing the door very quietly behind her, making her oblivious to the Executioner until she turned to head for the stairs.

Their eyes locked.

A heartbeat passed before she turned and rushed toward the casement window at the far end of the hallway. Bolan tore after her, holstering the pistol as muscled legs pistoned him down the hall. She hadn't done anything wrong, at least not that Bolan knew, which meant she shouldn't have had any reason to run. Her mode of dress and attempt to leave the apartment undetected spoke volumes about her profession. If she was prostituting on these streets, then that meant she worked for one of Chico's boys.

That made her a valuable commodity indeed where Bolan was concerned.

Bolan reached the casement window and launched his body through it. He noticed the overhead railing of the fire escape and grabbed it to keep from diving headfirst off the building. He dropped gracefully to the horizontal platform and looked to see the woman had nearly reached the bottom. The Executioner pursued her, intent to not let her out of his sight. If she managed to escape him, he'd be back to square one.

The chase continued from the back of the building to the street and down the sidewalk of Love Row. The woman looked lithe and agile, but she proved no match against the superior speed and strength of the Executioner. Within half a block he closed a significant gap between them. Hunter and quarry raced up the sidewalk until the woman reached an intersection and turned to dash kitty-corner through it. Bolan poured on the steam, intent she wouldn't progress far beyond the opposing curb.

The clipped, steady sound of pistol reports and subsequent buzz of rounds past his head changed Bolan's mind. The warrior looked in every direction and quickly saw the source

The Reader Service — Here's how it works:

Accepting your 2 free books and free gift (gift valued at approximately $5.00) places you under no obligation to buy anything. You may keep the books and gift and return the shipping statement marked "cancel." If you do not cancel, about a month later we'll send you 6 additional books and bill you just $31.94* — that's a savings of 24% off the cover price of all 6 books! And there's no extra charge for shipping! You may cancel at any time, but if you choose to continue, every other month we'll send you 6 more books, which you may either purchase at the discount price or return to us and cancel your subscription.

*Terms and prices subject to change without notice. Price does not include applicable taxes. Sales tax applicable in N.Y. Canadian residents will be charged applicable provincial taxes and GST. Offer not valid in Quebec. Credit or debit balances in a customer's account(s) may be offset by any other outstanding balance owed by or to the customer. Offer available while quantities last.

If offer card is missing write to: The Reader Service, P.O. Box 1867, Buffalo NY 14240-1867

NO POSTAGE
NECESSARY
IF MAILED
IN THE
UNITED STATES

BUSINESS REPLY MAIL
FIRST-CLASS MAIL   PERMIT NO. 717   BUFFALO, NY

POSTAGE WILL BE PAID BY ADDRESSEE

THE READER SERVICE
PO BOX 1867
BUFFALO NY 14240-9952

Get FREE BOOKS and a FREE GIFT when you play the...

LAS VEGAS
GAME

Just scratch off the gold box with a coin. Then check below to see the gifts you get! →

YES!

I have scratched off the gold box. Please send me my **2 FREE BOOKS** and **gift for which I qualify**. I understand that I am under no obligation to purchase any books as explained on the back of this card.

366 ADL E4CE   **166 ADL E4CE**

FIRST NAME   LAST NAME

ADDRESS

APT.#   CITY

STATE/PROV.   ZIP/POSTAL CODE

7	7	7	Worth TWO FREE BOOKS plus a BONUS Mystery Gift!
🍒	🍒	🍒	Worth TWO FREE BOOKS!
🔔	🔔	♣	TRY AGAIN!

Offer limited to one per household and not valid to current subscribers of Gold Eagle® books. All orders subject to approval. Please allow 4 to 6 weeks for delivery.

of the shooting—a young Hispanic male in ratty blue jeans hanging below his waist line and a filthy tank top. The man held his pistol sideways as he walked in Bolan's direction. The Executioner never broke stride, instead leveling the Beretta at his opponent and squeezing the trigger on the run. The pistol produced more of a cough than much else as he had loaded 125-grain subsonic cartridges. Both 9 mm slugs punched through the hood's chest, leaving behind small, red splotches. The impact knocked him flat to his back—he was dead before he hit the street.

Bolan caught the woman a minute later and dragged her to a quick stop. The viselike hand that clamped on her biceps caused her to emit a yelp. The Executioner eased off some but not so much that she could get away. He saw her eyes go wide at the sight of his pistol, so he opted to put it away. There seemed little point in trying to intimidate her into giving him the information he wanted. Maybe, just maybe, if she perceived he didn't pose any threat to her she might be persuaded to cooperate with him.

"Let me go!" she screamed, beating on his chest and shoulders. "Let me go, you asshole!"

She tried to knee him in the groin, but Bolan evaded by sidestepping and pinning her to the wall with his forearm. "Take it easy. I'm not here to hurt you, I just want some information."

"I don't give a shit!" she said. "You better let me go or you'll have to deal with Chico."

Bingo. "So you do know Charles Camano. Well, that puts to rest any doubts I might have had."

The expression in her eyes told Bolan the prostitute knew she'd messed up good. He hadn't said a word about Camano, aka Chico, and yet here she'd managed to let on that she not only knew him but also worked for him. Being she was a prostitute and understanding Chico's modus operandi, the Executioner figured nearly all the women who worked for the scumbag were probably sampled like merchandise first by the big boss himself. That would make her and every one of her colleagues intimate with a number of Chico's operations.

"There are two ways we can play this," Bolan continued. "You can answer my questions and walk away, or—"

"Or you can take me downtown," she said. "Yeah, I've heard this shit before, cop, so there's no point in wasting your breath."

"Actually, I'm not a cop so you haven't heard this before," Bolan countered darkly. "The alternative to not talking to me is much more unpleasant than a trip downtown."

She studied him a moment, then replied, "What's your business with Chico?"

"It's just that, *my* business."

"I talk to you, I'm dead."

The Executioner shook his head. "Not likely. I'm here to put Chico out of work. Permanently. That means you and everyone else in this part of town will have to start looking for gainful employment somewhere else, preferably with legit establishments."

His statement generated a scoffing laugh. "Ha, that's rich! We all got contracts with Chico, enforced by his guys and unbreakable. He knows people everywhere, pal. Nobody gets out. Hear me? Something happens to him, someone else will just step up in his place and we'll all be right back here shaking our asses for the customers."

"You have contracts enforced by his guys." Bolan jerked his head toward the lifeless, bleeding body of the gangbanger in the street. "Like him?"

She finally turned to notice the corpse and inhaled sharply. She'd been so intent on getting away she'd been totally oblivious to the results of the man's encounter with Bolan. He could see it visibly shook her resolve, and he could see just a glimmer of hope behind her eyes, as if maybe someone had finally demonstrated that others could stand up against Chico and actually win.

"What's your name?" Bolan asked. "Your real name?"

"Missy," she blurted, her East Coast accent suddenly gone.

He eased off the pressure of holding her against the wall and in a gentler voice said, "Look, Missy, you don't have to spend the rest of your life in the dregs. You have options, ways to make a better life for yourself. You want to know my business with Chico? It's to put him and MS-13 *out* of business. You got that? So now is your chance to help out yourself and others. Tell me where I can find him."

Missy looked at the body, looked back at the Executioner and replied, "All right, I'll talk to you. But on one condition."

"Name it," Bolan replied.

And she did.

12

Under normal circumstances, Bolan would never have allowed a young woman to talk him into what Missy proposed. But these weren't normal circumstances.

Time to put down MS-13 and pick up Cristobal's tail was short, and in turn so likely was the life of Ignacio Paz. Missy had been to Charlie Camano's residence, just as the Executioner suspected, and she convinced him the only way he could get inside would be to pose as a pimp looking for a job. Bolan wondered at first about her motivation until Missy told him of her younger sister, the chief reason she worked in the profession she did, and even took him to meet her.

The young, dirty-faced girl couldn't have been more than half Missy's age. She was quiet and unassuming and looked at Bolan with frightened eyes. Missy stayed in a run-down tenement on the west side of Love Row along with others like her, which is where she'd been heading during her flight from Bolan. The girl, whose name was Samantha, didn't say more than two words to Bolan the entire time. Missy excused herself to draw a bath for the girl and then returned to where she left Bolan seated, which served as TV room, playroom and dining room. Only a half wall separated that single room from the kitchen.

Bolan had noticed the peeling paint on the walls, the holes patched with drywall compound, the dust and decay of the room in general. He also took note of the meager furnishings. The top of a dilapidated TV tray had been mounted atop a flimsy wooden crate and now served as a sort of play table for the little girl; crayons, a couple of tattered books and dress-up doll that was missing an arm adorned it. The television had rabbit ears and looked to be at least twenty years old. Bolan doubted it even worked, seeing as there was no digital converter box in sight.

When Missy returned from the bathroom, Bolan reached into his pocket and withdrew all the cash he had, a small amount he'd pulled from the massive funds of his war chest. He set it on the scarred, dinette table and looked Missy in the eyes.

"There's about ten thousand dollars there," he said. "It's yours."

"I don't need charity," she replied immediately and padded into the kitchen.

Bolan stood and followed her to the kitchen entrance where he leaned against the wall and folded his arms. "It's not charity, it's payment."

She stopped and eyed him suspiciously. "For what?"

"Helping me get to Chico."

That brought a smile to her lips. "You sure that's all you're looking for?"

"I'm not interested in sampling your personal wares, if that's the implication," Bolan said. "That money's more than enough to give you a new start. I meant what I said about getting you out of here, taking the chance to start over."

Missy appeared to think about his words but then didn't say anything else. Instead, she turned and busied herself pulling a frying pan from a cupboard next to the stove, and withdrawing some eggs and a slab of bacon from the refrigerator.

"Do you want something?" she asked Bolan without looking at him.

He declined and then said, "I'm altering our deal a bit."

"In what way?"

"I'll let you get me inside Chico's place and make the intros. But once that's done, you take your sister and that money and you split. No arguments, no questions."

"And if I refuse?"

"Then we have no deal."

Missy shook her head. "And you have no prize, big man."

Bolan offered a cold smile. "I have other ways of getting to Chico."

Missy finished making the eggs and poured Bolan a cup of coffee; she picked the stack of bills off the table and studied them before dropping them on the table with an exaggerated smack. She turned and started to head for the bathroom where she'd left her sister, and then seemed to think better of it and returned to sweep the bills off the table. Then she disappeared down the hall once more. Bolan took it all in stride, believing it was her way of saying she found his terms agreeable.

When she returned a minute later she put Samantha at the table and set the eggs and bacon in front of her with a plastic spoon. She left again and a minute later Bolan heard the shower running. It surprised him at first, the fact she had entrusted the care of her sister to him, but then he realized it was a sign he'd made headway with her. She at least trusted him so far as to believe his intentions were nonpunitive, and that had to count for something—especially someone with her background.

Ten minutes passed before Missy returned, and Bolan scented the flowery hint of her shampoo. She cleaned up rather nicely, and she possessed a natural beauty beneath all the heavy makeup. Obviously the frizzy blond hair had been a wig, as the hair she'd combed out was more strawberry in color and bounced off her slim shoulders in waves. Without the heavy mascara and eyeliner, he could see the sea blue of her eyes, almost like a sparkling aquamarine. The blue jeans shorts she wore were faded but hugged the curves of her hips quite nicely, and Bolan could tell that she couldn't have been more than twenty-two or twenty-three.

Bolan felt helpless not to comment. "That's a much better look."

She grinned and wrinkled her nose. "Yeah?"

He nodded and smiled. "It suits you."

Missy inclined her head in acceptance of his compliment. They studied each other for a long moment before she noticed his cup was empty and took it into the kitchen to pour him a fresh helping. She set it in front of him and then folded her arms and leaned against the wall. Bolan watched her watching him.

Over the brim of his cup, he said, "You want to ask me something?"

She shrugged and then reached out and fiddled with her sister's hair. "I got to wondering, if you're not a cop why did you even bother to come here. What are you really up to?"

"I can't tell you that," Bolan replied.

"I figured."

"Not exactly," he continued quickly. "The fact is, if I told you everything about me and my reasons for being here, your life wouldn't be worth anything."

"That's funny, since from the moment I met you I sort of had that impression already."

"I'm not talking about me. I'm not a threat to you. But simply knowledge of me or my operation alone poses enough risks to you. If I tell you more and the enemy gets its hands on you, well, I don't need to tell you what they'll do to you if they think you're withholding information." Bolan nodded at Samantha and added, "Or your loved ones."

"If the enemy gets its hands on me?" She arched an eyebrow. "You talk about them like you're at war."

"I am," the Executioner replied grimly.

Missy didn't have a reply for that one, and Bolan surmised it was because she hadn't expected him to say it. The facts were what they were, though, and Bolan knew there wasn't a thing he could do to change it. But one thing the warrior had learned was if he could make a difference in the life of even one victim—and Missy had been victimized by the machinations of tyrants like Camano and Cristobal whether she thought so or not—his altruism could have a snowball effect. Maybe not here or now, but Missy would remember his generosity and perhaps find a way to pay it forward to someone else. Eventually, it would come back around and put men like the shot-callers in MS-13 permanently out of business.

"What do you plan to do with Sam while we're gone?"

"She can stay here," Missy said with a shrug. "She'll be safe. Nobody in Chico's outfit knows where I live, not even Chico himself."

"Don't be too sure about that," Bolan said. "I think for the time she might be safer with a friend of mine."

Missy studied him. "You wouldn't take her away from me, would you?"

"It wouldn't benefit her and it wouldn't benefit you. She's family, the only family it seems you have left." In a wistful tone Bolan added, "I wouldn't ever split up a family unless it became absolutely necessary. But with what we're getting into, believe me when I say she'll be safer where nobody can reach her."

Missy looked at Samantha, who had eaten only about a quarter of what was on her plate and was now playing with the rest. "Would you like to go on a little trip, Sam?"

Sam looked at Missy and then at Bolan, who smiled at her. She studied the icy eyes of the Executioner and had to have seen something there. Children were intuitive, Bolan believed, with an innate sense for discerning the good guys from the bad. She obviously saw something in Bolan she trusted, which meant a lot, considering Missy might very well have had boy-friends in the past who were likely not of exceptional caliber in the area of responsible manhood.

"You can meet my friend," Bolan said. "You'll really like him. His name is Jack."

MISSY PACKED an overnight bag for her sister and herself, then Bolan drove the pair to the airport outside Los Angeles. Before he and Missy set out for Camano's palatial estate on the northeast fringes of the city, he left Grimaldi with strict instructions of what to do with Samantha in the event neither of them returned.

Bolan took a note of interest that Camano had chosen to live close to his operations. Men like him normally made a point of keeping themselves distanced from the work, either under advice of their high-priced attorneys or because deep down they didn't really have the stomach for it. Then again, Chico hadn't exactly been born with a silver spoon in his mouth. According to his dossier, he came into the country as a small child, just one of the many refugees of the civil war in El Salvador. His mother had only been able to obtain the status of a legal alien but, because she was able to prove Chico's father was an American newsman, it proved less difficult for Chico to obtain U.S. citizenship. Eventually, his status as a citizen would have earned the same right for his mother, but she died suddenly of cholera when he was still a tot.

The L.A. news reporter who had sired Chico never believed the lad was his son even though the paternity test proved he was. He agreed to take the boy into his house, but shortly thereafter he lost his job. A down-on-his-luck newsman— with a sullied reputation for being a boozer—didn't make for a great role model as a parent. Like so many other kids with similar stories of a broken home life, Camano turned to the only place left he could for help: MS-13. The gang gave him structure, a purpose and discipline, in some corrupted sense, and Bolan could understand that because he'd seen it more times than he cared to count.

Like the shot-callers before him, Chico rose through the ranks until he'd carved his own little piece out of the poverty and denigration of East L.A. He enlisted the members of other Hispanic gangs until they could no longer compete, or trampled them by undercutting prices. He forged alliances with MS-13 shot-callers in surrounding communities, establishing his reputation as a fair but ruthless businessman until nobody dared cross the invisible lines he'd painted to mark the boundaries of his vast territory.

Eventually, Chico created his new empire based mostly on sex and drugs, and built the place called Love Row from the ground up.

"His crews, he calls them soldier ants, roam the streets day and night," Missy explained between snapping her gum. "But then you know that, since you ran into one of them when you were chasing me."

"So Chico calls them soldier ants." He looked at her with a wicked glint. "You see, even *he* thinks it's a war."

Missy nodded thoughtfully as she stared straight ahead. "Yeah, I see your point."

"What else can you tell me about him?"

"Well, it used to be we were pretty much free agents. There was a time when Chico ran all the action personally, but then I think it got too big for one guy to handle so he started to hire these guys he calls juniors."

"Pimps," Bolan said.

Missy nodded once. "Yeah, that's basically what they are…glorified pimps. But in Chico's operations they act more like business managers. Most of them are okay to work with. You know? There's just a bad apple every now and again who gets off on slapping you around a bit. But Chico isn't into that. He thinks it's bad business, draws the cops and whatever, and he doesn't like anyone damaging merchandise. Juniors who slap the girls around aren't long for this world."

"So did you work the streets or for this escort service he's fronting with the nonprofit business?"

"Both. We trade off because the perks with the escort service are so much better. Nice dresses, big parties where you get to rub elbows with the Hollywood types. All the johns are older, some who can't even get it up, but they want a trophy on their arm more than anything else. Everybody knows what we *really* do for our customers, but nobody says anything about it. You speak up about the services of Love Row you'll have Chico to answer to, and everybody knows it. So we all keep our mouths shut and the juniors make sure things run smoothly."

"What about the drugs?"

"Most of the time they get placed with an order for the girls," she replied. "You see, most of these old blowhards just want to sample the glitzy life. A lot are from out of town, maybe college kids looking to dip their wicks. Most of the time, though, they're businessmen or corporate types who want to live it up for one evening, you know…like take risks and stuff. I guess because they don't live on the wild side most of the time the idea of fooling around on their wives or doing something illegal adds to the excitement of it all."

She reached into her small handbag and withdrew a pack of cigarettes. She started to light one, then asked Bolan if he minded. He shook his head, and she fired up before cracking her window. She took a long drag and blew the smoke toward the crack before continuing. "They're mostly harmless, those guys. It's the locals down on Love Row that make this job more dangerous."

"You sound almost as if you like it."

Missy didn't say anything at first. She shrugged, took another drag and then replied, "It's what I know. After my parents died, I had to find a way to support Sam. At eighteen, I didn't have any real job skills or the tits to make most pigs who would hire me overlook that fact."

Bolan only nodded. What could he say? It wasn't like he could pretend he hadn't heard that same story a million times before. Bolan had come to accept that while he might know about the many ills of the world, his mission didn't call for him to cure them all. Nor would he have attempted to try even if he thought he had a chance of a modicum of success. He'd built his principles of War Everlasting on the belief that if he concentrated his efforts on the source of the vice that he could topple the criminal empire. He'd proved it with the Mafia, dealing them a major blow, and in a similar way it had worked against terrorism.

It didn't work every time and Bolan was enough of a pragmatist to know such expectations were unrealistic. He also knew *this* plan came with risks, considerable risks to Missy and if something happened to her, little Samantha would be truly orphaned. Bolan would make sure it didn't come to that. If things went hard, he'd make sure Missy got clear; every minute they were inside Chico's estate together meant another minute she posed a liability to the Executioner's mission, but he'd agreed to her terms and she'd agreed to his. They had a deal.

"Just make sure you play your part convincingly today or we're both dead," Bolan reminded her.

The Executioner drove the rental into the neighborhood and eventually they arrived at Chico's house. It wasn't quite the palace he'd originally envisioned, but just one of the many nice homes lining the spotless streets. All was trimmed hedges and manicured lawns; spotless curbs where numbers were painted clearly in front of each property. If Bolan hadn't known better, he would have thought it looked like any other white, upper class neighborhood in the City of Angels suburbia, maybe even offshore West Coast area or Hollywood.

Bolan swung the nose of the vehicle into the drive, stopped in front of the massive pair of wrought-iron gates and stabbed the button on the call box. A moment later a voice answered gruffly at the same time Bolan noticed the pair of motorized cameras on either side of the gate angle down on them.

"Yeah?"

Missy leaned forward and yelled, "We need to see Chico."

"You got an appointment, Missy?" the voice demanded.

"No, but he'll see us. Just tell him it's me."

"Okay," the voice replied. "But who's your boyfriend?"

"Just stop playing twenty fucking questions and tell Chico we need to see him!" Missy snapped.

There was no reply to that, but Bolan looked with some surprise at her. Missy didn't say anything to him. He noticed the East Coast accent had returned, and she was now chomping her gum. It was as if she had transformed instantaneously into the street hooker he'd first grabbed up a few hours before, and for a moment the Executioner thought someone had switched her out with the real Missy when he wasn't looking.

Less than a minute elapsed before six men suddenly appeared at the front gate. They were all big, mean-looking types wearing loafers, chinos and nice shirts; wicked submachine guns slung over their shoulders. Bolan couldn't be sure if they were security or a killing team, they really could have filled either role with little difficulty.

As the wrought-iron gates swung inward automatically, the

crew fanned out and covered the car with the guns. The
speaker issued a hiss but nothing more. Then they were being
pulled out of the car and frisked. Bolan allowed them to
relieve him of the Colt .45 automatic pistol he'd traded out
for his Beretta 93-R. Being a military pistol with some significant specialty modifications, Bolan didn't want to risk
being taken for the hardened specialist he was rather than just
an out-of-work hired gun. He'd also elected not to bring any
firepower with him in the vehicle, trunk or otherwise. That
would have marked him for sure.

They patted down Missy, too—with much enthusiasm
while maintaining a bit of professional decorum. They didn't
take chances. Then they were escorted up to the gate and
their vehicle left there at the curb, keys in the hands of one of
the security guys. Bolan marked the man's face and watched
carefully as the guy dropped the keys in his pocket.

Just in case he had to get them back in a hurry.

Then the six gunners escorted them up the long, winding
drive and toward the den of Charles Camano, aka Chico. A
den where Bolan knew the lion waited. And he had to wonder
if they would ever be coming out.

13

Ignacio Paz didn't believe in reincarnation—he'd been raised Catholic.

But he had to wonder for a moment if he'd done something bad enough in a former life that he was now paying for it in this one. Despite the hush money he paid, word had traveled very quickly about his little encounter with the drunken patron at the cantina, and before long four guys in nice clothes wearing pistols showed up to talk to him. Paz wouldn't have even known if it hadn't been for a call from Arturo, his faithful friend at the front desk, saying they were on their way.

And they had a key.

That's when Paz grabbed everything that might identify him, including the Glock 21 pistol with the filed-off serial number, and jumped out the second-story window of his room, which he'd chosen due to the fact it led onto the roof of the back patio. The roof was flimsy, made of old fiberboard that creaked and cracked under his weight. As Paz made it off the back, the first of his quartet of followers jumped out the window after him. He was a big guy, and St. Jude had to have heard Paz's prayer because the man went right through that roof and crashed into the flimsier floorboards of the enclosed back porch.

Bless Arturo and that goddamned cheap-ass roof, Paz thought.

The undercover agent made the back alley and raced along it, slipping once in a mud puddle that hadn't completely dried from one of the recent rains. He didn't bother to even check his six. If they weren't pursuing him right at that moment, it wouldn't be long before they were. Serafin Cristobal had his fingers into everything here; everyone informed on everybody, and Paz had to wonder if anyplace in all of San Salvador would be safe.

Well, he did know of *one* place, and for now he'd have to trust his instincts and go there. Mariana wouldn't be happy to see him, but she was a nice kid—a clean kid with two small babies to think of—who wouldn't give him up to the likes of Cristobal. He'd asked her to come back with him, offered to use his pull in the government to get her into the States on an H-1B work visa, but she adamantly refused him. She pointed out all the good reasons. He was married and there was no way in hell his wife would share the goods. Not to mention El Salvador was her home. How would he feel if she'd asked him to give up the only life he'd ever known to stay there with her? Would he renounce his citizenship? Would he be willing to be a part of her life there and the life of her babies?

Hell, maybe if she had asked him at a more opportune time his answer would have been yes, but now there wasn't any way in hell he could agree to such terms. The head of the largest and most powerful gang force in the whole country was onto him now, and it wouldn't be long before he had a price on his head. Every wannabe who desired to ingratiate themselves with Cristobal would be out looking for him, ready to deliver him to the inner sanctums of Le Gango Jefe himself.

It wouldn't be long before the word got out, anyway. Cristobal would want him just on general principles, and he couldn't afford that. Hell, he doubted his life would be worth much at all before the day ended. Yeah, by the time the sun set Paz's very existence would be endangered. This was their world and he'd become the quarry for the prey, the lamb to Cristobal's lion.

And there wasn't a damn thing he could do about it.

THE INTERIOR DECOR of the estate hardly seemed in line with the tastes of a vice kingpin with Camano's reputation.

Bolan noted that fine artwork adorned the walls, and in one room Bolan caught a glimpse of ceramic busts. The Executioner was obviously dealing with a man of exquisite tastes, but something seemed out of place. Camano had been raised on the streets of one of the toughest, most violent cities in the country and yet here he'd chosen to grace his home with artwork of reputed origins and decorate with a light, airy touch.

It didn't make any sense and for some oddball reason— Bolan couldn't put his finger on it—it chilled the sheen of sweat on the back of his neck and sent alarm bells ringing through his internal sensory network. The security entourage led them to the back of the property, through a sliding glass door and onto a patio that overlooked grounds tended with the same immaculacy as the interior. Redolent flowers, shining splendidly in the noonday sun, crowded the fresh sod beds alongside the five-foot brick walls on either side, and a collage of vines and creepers wound their way through latticework stationed along the back property line.

A large, dark-haired male sat at a patio table in a fancy lawn chair, sipping from a tumbler filled with amber-colored liquid over cracked ice and puffing from what Bolan surmised could only be one of Cuba's finest. His fingers were thick, stumpy like those of an obese man, and yet he didn't seem to have a lick of fat anywhere. He wore a collared silk shirt, open at the chest by several buttons, which showed just enough to make the definition in his chest and abdominal muscles obvious. He had a Fu Manchu-style mustache and the stubble of a beard grazed his prominent chin. His eyes were deeply inset, beady like a rat's, but the rest of his face was dark and smooth.

Bolan made out the nuances that differentiated his ethnicity. To the untrained eye he would have been described as Hispanic, but the Executioner spotted the very Central American features and would have immediately guessed he was from Honduras or Guatemala. Or El Salvador. The impassive expression, almost smug, gave away his position in the hierarchy as did the behavior of the four additional men posted very near to him. Bodyguards.

"Missy!" He held out his hand and she stepped away from Bolan to bend over and kiss the solid row of gold rings on his fingers. "It's nice to see you, girl."

Missy smiled and stepped back. "Long time, Chico."

"No, *too* long." He tapped his lap with a massive palm and gestured for her to take a seat. She looked hesitant at first but covered the moment nicely by smiling and accepting his invitation. She leaned close—wrapping her arms around his neck—whispered something in his ear and he immediately giggled under his breath. A criminal overlord giggling? The entire exchange seemed almost surreal, but Bolan kept silent. Finally, Missy directed his attention to her escort.

"Chico, I'd like you to meet Mike Grecki."

Using his usual cover wasn't wise, since he was pretty certain there was word over the wire already regarding his exploits in Herndon. They would be on guard, and Bolan suspected Cristobal would have spread the word to all of the other branches. The big problem would be to decide what information to get to which groups, since they would still be trying to recover from Bolan's initial blitz. The very fact that their size made them more powerful and efficient than an average gang was also a weakness Bolan sought to exploit.

"Grecki, eh?" Chico looked at one of his men and then locked eyes with Bolan. "And what's your story?"

"Just a friend of Missy's," Bolan replied evenly, cautious to maintain a respectful tone. The behavioral profile from Stony Man indicated Camano was prone to bouts of violent temper, and anything might set him off. It seemed almost unjustified given the man who now sat before him, calm with an almost mischievous twinkle in his expression, but Bolan didn't rely on that. Surface impressions were usually the most dangerous, and Stony Man's intelligence was rarely inaccurate. Better to wait to see what the guy had to say.

"A friend?" He looked at Missy. "That right, girl?"

Missy nodded and cracked her gum, and then said, "I ran into him over by the Row."

"Heh." Camano looked Bolan in the eyes. "You know that's MS-13 territory, pal. That makes it *my* territory, *vato,* and nobody down there does business without my say so. Understand?"

Bolan remained silent, expressionless and watchful for any telltale signs things were going to go hard. He looked around him, quickly took in distances and sizes, watched for who held their weapons a bit too casually and might be easy to overpower if the need came down. He then turned his eyes back on Camano and waited for the hood to continue.

"Quiet boy," the porn and drug kingpin added. "Don't say much, eh? Strong and silent type, is that it? Missy, why you bring this white boy here, anyway?"

"I need work," Bolan said.

Camano looked at him and his eyes narrowed. "I wasn't talking to you."

He turned back to Missy. "Eh, why you bring him here?"

"He helped me out, Chico," she said. "Be nice to the guy, okay? Some dudes came down, those shitheads from La Eme, and started roughing me up. He stepped in to help me."

"He helped you, eh? Why you need this dude's help,

huh? I got my boys down there. Where was Pedro? What about Emilio?"

"They shot him, Chico! They shot Emilio!" Missy turned on the waterworks then and began to visibly quake. "They killed him for no reason. He was coming to help and they killed him. Then Mike here showed up and stopped them. They ran when they saw him coming, shooting at them."

Camano gestured to one of the men standing behind him and he stepped forward instantly. "You know anything about this?" he asked. When the enforcer shook his head he told him, "Check it out, now. I want to know where Emilio is."

The guy nodded and then turned and disappeared into the house. Camano turned his attention back to Bolan. The warrior stood stock-still, not moving or flinching, just waiting for it to sink in a bit. He knew if the boss didn't buy their story the gig would turn sour real quick, and then they would be up the proverbial creek without a paddle. Bolan meant to ensure that Missy got out of it alive, just as he'd vowed before they came in, even if he had to overpower one of these security detail guys and deal another crushing blow to the MS-13 empire here and now. It wouldn't get him any closer to finding Cristobal or Ignacio Paz, but at least he'd remove one more piece of filth from the world.

Guys like Camano were part of a criminal surplus America could do without.

"So why bring him to me?"

"I didn't, really," Missy said. "I got him to bring me to you. I was scared, Chico!"

The shot-caller stroked his mustache for a time, thinking about what he'd been told, processing and calculating. Finally he said, "It's been a hell of a while since La Eme tried to muscle me. Why would they pick now to do it?"

Bolan's instinct told him to gamble so he played his ace card. "Maybe they heard about the trouble back east."

Camano's eyes hardened and he looked Bolan straight in the eye. "What do you know about that, white boy, eh?"

"Look, Chico," Bolan said, "no disrespect, but I helped out your lady friend here and I brought her to you on good terms. I'd like to leave the same way if you don't mind. I don't go for this kind of treatment when doing people favors."

"Yeah, well, I appreciate you helping one of my women," Camano replied. "But you best know you're here on my terms. That means you leave when I say. You feel me?"

Bolan thought about pressing a bit more but then thought better of it. "Fine with me. I'll just wait out here and enjoy your hospitality."

"Yeah, you do that." He looked at Missy who cocked her head, chomping her gum and eyeballing him with a look that said she didn't much approve of his attitude. He seemed to soften some and said, "Okay, Missy, I give this boy a chance because of you. Why don't you fix yourself something? You want a drink, Grecki?"

Bolan nodded and Missy got up to do the bidding. She walked straight to the portable wet bar against the wall, almost as if she knew right where it was. Bolan's suspicions heightened, and he wondered if he hadn't given appropriate credit to MS-13.

Maybe they already had him made and set a trap by using Missy as bait.

First, Missy had originally acted as if she'd only had a single encounter with Chico—a sort of initiation into the fold—and yet here the two were chatting it up like old friends. Second, she seemed to know her way around pretty well, considering she'd only been here once. Last, it seemed like she'd fallen into her role a little too easily, and the transformation he'd witnessed before admittedly spooked him a bit. On the other hand, there were a few things remiss in his theory. If she had actually planned to betray him, then why all the pretext, the checking on the now deceased Emilio and such? They could have just as easily ambushed him when he walked in. And then there was her hesitation when he invited her to sit on his lap, and all the crocodile tears acting like she was scared. They had cooked up the story together about her being accosted by members of a rival gang, sure, but she hadn't mentioned anything about employing the theatrics he just witnessed. Besides, Jack was overseeing to the safety of her sister. If she planned to betray him, she wouldn't have left herself in such a compromising position. She had more brains than that. The Executioner had gone into this deciding to trust her, and now he needed to see it through and bury assumptions. She'd brought him inside this tight circle, and now it was do or die, with no time to second-guess her tactics. It rankled him a bit, as he was used to having complete control over any given situation, but he'd gone into this one with the full knowledge he'd have to play much of this tune by ear.

Missy returned a minute later and handed him a glass. He nodded in thanks and waited until she took a seat in a chair next to Camano before raising his glass and nodding a silent toast. Camano returned the nod, almost imperceptibly, and Bolan took a whiff even as he put the drink to his lips. He detected no presence of alcohol, just tonic water. That cinched it for him: Missy was definitely on his side.

Camano still didn't offer Bolan a seat, but the Executioner decided to let that fact pass him by. After all, the crime boss had no reason to trust him and especially not under the current circumstances. He noticed Camano hadn't inquired further into Bolan's comment about what had transpired back in Herndon other than to ask how he'd known about it, a subject Bolan had managed to avoid by turning the conversation around and putting Camano on the defensive.

The guy Camano had sent to check out their story emerged onto the patio and when their eyes made contact the guy nodded.

Camano turned to Bolan. "Looks like you were telling the truth. You sure they were La Eme?"

Bolan nodded toward Missy and said, "This isn't my usual territory, so if Missy says they were, then that's good enough for me."

"Okay, so I guess we're going to need to explain to our friends on the other side of town once more that Love Row is off-limits to them. And I suppose you're looking for some sort of handout, eh?"

Bolan shrugged. "Not necessarily. I could use the work."

"Yeah, well, not until I check you out," he said. "And not until you're initiated. For now, I think we keep you around here for a time until something comes up."

"But Chico, who's going to take me back?"

"Why you want to go back there? You just damn near lost your ass there, Missy."

"Because I got to work tonight," Missy whined.

"All right, I'll have a couple of the boys drive you home. But Grecki will have to stay here for a while so we can get better acquainted." For the first time since they had arrived, Camano smiled and Bolan noted a lower tooth of gold flash. "Maybe I can find some use for him after all."

Bolan took note of the ominous tone in Camano's reply but remained silent. The guy continued to study him with those beady eyes, the hint of a smug grin playing on the lips between the ridiculous mustache, and for a moment the Executioner had to fight the urge to push his face in. Such a reaction would surely result in his death, as well as that of Missy's, and accomplish nothing. For now, he'd play along.

And at least Missy had honored their agreement by getting them to drive her home.

Soon, though, Bolan would make his move.

Yeah…soon.

RIGHT AT THAT MOMENT, Ignacio Paz felt nothing like Tigre Garra originally envisioned by Gary Marciano. He'd been given that code name because his government intended for him to be just like the claws of a tiger, reaching into his prey quickly and purposefully to rip its heart out. Instead, Paz managed to get what seemed like half of Cristobal's army on his tail, and he didn't see any real way to get out of it with his neck intact.

Or those of Mariana and her children.

Against his better judgment, Paz had gone to the woman's house and beat on her door incessantly until she finally agreed to open it. Paz had to admit he was grateful to her, but he had hardly expected things to spiral so quickly out of control. She stood in the kitchen now, watching him as he hungrily devoured the shredded pork spiced with red and green chilies wrapped in sunbaked tortillas. He washed it all down with an ice cold beer. As he went into the fridge for a second, Mariana closed the door, just missing his hand, and eyed him with unmistakable disdain.

"What has happened to you, Erasmo?" she asked, using the cover name he'd given her.

"Nothing you need to worry about."

"It is *him,* isn't it?" she demanded. She began to beat on his chest. "How could you do this? How could you risk them following you here and putting my babies in danger?"

She stormed to the front door of her shack, a hovel, really, that somehow passed for a home, and started to open the door. "I want you to leave—"

Paz jumped from the kitchen to where she stood, shoved her onto the couch and kicked the door close as he hollered, "Santa Maria, keep that damn door closed, woman! You trying to get us all killed?"

The next moment it proved a moot question as the window next to the door imploded and sent glass shards flying in all directions. The object that shattered the glass bounced off the thin carpet runner leading from the door, a wicker of flame issuing from one end, and then struck the flimsy metal of a bookcase and broke open. Paz leaped toward Mariana and knocked her off the seat as the gasoline of the Molotov cocktail ignited and whooshed up the bookcase to ignite a number of the books. More gasoline ran toward the carpet, and a moment later it went up in flames.

Paz checked to make sure Mariana was unhurt and then yanked her to her feet and pushed her past the increasing fire toward the back room where she'd put her two kids down for a nap. Simultaneously Paz drew the Glock pistol from beneath his shirt and looked over his shoulder. Pockets of smoke were already starting to fill the front room as the old, dry timbers of the house caught and the fire spread quickly, hungrily, as if bent on consuming everything in its path as quickly as possible.

Yeah, it acted much like the empire of Serafin Cristobal— Le Gango Jefe was a man bent on dominance, bent on eating up everything that stood in his way. Paz had wondered how much was enough? When did a man get enough money or power or prestige before he became as empty and lifeless as the domain he had built? Paz had been reared by Catholic parents who taught him it wasn't money, but the love thereof, that was the root of all evil. Now seeing what was happening, that someone would so callously disregard the life of women and children, he understood the platitude.

Paz grabbed the toddler and jarred him from sleep. He

began to cry, but the infant seemed to be more resilient as he hardly stirred when Mariana scooped him from his crib. He tried to lift the window, but it had been painted shut. He searched frantically until the solution presented itself, a pillow covered by a ratty but clean pillow case. Paz placed it against the window and firmly punched the pillow at its center. The thin glass gave underneath the force, and Paz was able to easily clear the remaining shards with quick taps from the pistol butt. He took the infant from Mariana and nodded for her to go out first, then handed the two children to her once she was through.

"Run, Mariana!" he told her. "Get as far away from here as you can! If anybody asks, you don't know me. You *never* knew me."

"Erasmo, I—"

"I know what you're going to say. And don't. It's better if you forget we ever met."

Paz felt as if his heart might explode from his chest as he watched her tromp away, barefoot, over the ruts and imperfections of what passed for her backyard but really amounted to nothing more than a mud hole. He waited until she was out of sight and then turned to face the front room. The smoke was thick now, so thick he knew he could spend only a few seconds going through it to get to the front door. He would throw himself into the path of his enemies, give Mariana a chance to get away.

They wouldn't pursue her—at least he prayed they wouldn't.

Cristobal's MS-13 thugs had come for Ignacio Paz.

And that's exactly what he intended to give them.

14

Once Missy was safely out of the picture, the Executioner began to formulate his plan. He would have to do it in two phases: first, take out Camano's security team and his protection goons, and second, hit the businesses on Love Row and make it look like La Eme, the competition, wasn't letting up. Through that, he could manipulate the situation and get close enough to take the MS-13 shot-caller out of the picture once and for all. Just like in Herndon, Bolan was confident L.A.'s finest could pick off any stragglers.

At first, no immediate opportunities came his way to get his gun back; it also looked like Camano had no intention of letting Bolan out of his sight. That scenario quickly faded in the mist of preparations for war. Camano's ambassador to the gang leader in La Eme returned with a message from the opposition's leadership swearing they had nothing to do with the killing of Emilio or invading Love Row to hassle a prostitute. Fortunately, Camano didn't buy it and Bolan added some tidbits to prime the pump.

"He's full of it," the warrior told Camano as they stood in the man's office inside the house. "I can describe all three of them, including the colors they were wearing and the hand signals they used."

"Anybody could read that shit on the Internet," Camano said. "I don't believe their homeboy that they weren't there trying to break into my action. They've been trying to do that for years. But that still don't explain why they did Emilio or why *you* were there."

"He shot at them first," Bolan replied easily.

"Say what?" interjected Camano's head ant, who everyone just called Flip, a nickname Bolan learned later was short for Felipe. "No way would he have done that."

Bolan eyed Flip. "He would if he was trying to protect Missy."

"Enough of this bullshit!" Camano hammered his desk with a big fist. "I'm not interested in who said what and who did shit, got it? I want to know who you are and what the fuck you was doing there. Or I swear, *pinche,* I will bust a cap on you myself!"

"Fine, fine!" Bolan held up his hands and said, "Your boss sent me."

It was a big chance, but Bolan figured he didn't have any other choice. He'd been thinking on Guerra's death quite a bit, and he just couldn't buy the Herndon shot-caller's hit had been the result of gang rivalry—blood was thick among gangs. No, the okay to hit Guerra had to come from much higher, most likely Serafin Cristobal, an order that stemmed from Bolan's theory Guerra had drawn way too much attention and lost control of the Herndon operations. It was no coincidence that Guerra had been executed and that the gang of a blood relative had followed Smalley with the sole purpose of exacting retribution. Why go to the trouble? So that meant there was yet another party with their finger in the pie, and Bolan had just bet the farm it was a freelancer.

Camano ordered everyone but Flip to clear the room. Once they were alone, Camano leaned back in his chair, folded his arms and studied Bolan through squinted eyes. He'd been trying to size him up, Bolan knew, figure out the Executioner's angles. Bolan had learned in such situations to never play out more line than absolutely necessary. He'd also learned the value of spinning bits and pieces rather than spinning a whole tale at one time. The larger the story, the more details to remember and the easier it was to get tripped up on the questions.

"Okay, you better talk fast, homeboy."

"Not much to say," Bolan replied easily. "I'm a freelancer. I've done work for him before."

"And who is *him* exactly? You say you work for my boss, then okay. You'll know his name."

Bolan looked at Flip and back at Camano. "I don't think so."

"Then you're a dead man because you're full of shit."

"You can threaten me all you want, but if you kill me the boss isn't going to be happy. I gave up my gun, showed your boys respect when I could have just as easily taken my chances banging heads with them. And I've answered all your questions up until now, but I don't drop names. Ever. Guerra's dead and I had the okay to do it. You're the favored one in all of this, so you don't have anything to worry about from me as long as you cooperate and keep things in control."

"Is that right?"

"That's right," Bolan shot back. "There's a guy with the Feds, some kind of special troubleshooter who just blew several major operations wide open back east. Word has it he's headed here next. He may already be here, in which case you're out of time. Especially if you decide to go to war with rivals instead of taking care of business."

"You think so?"

"I know so. Look, Chico, you want to kill me, then do it. I'm not afraid of you or death. But know that your boss sent me as a lifeline. I'd grab that, if I were you."

For a long time Camano kept silent, just stroked his Fu Manchu mustache and watched Bolan. He wasn't really staring at the Executioner, rather it seemed as if he were trying to look through him. Bolan didn't give quarter. He knew Chico would check into his story but that would take a bit of time, and Bolan planned to execute his plan before it made any difference. For the moment, he'd put Camano on the defensive, and he planned to keep him there until he could wrap things up in a nice, tidy package.

"Okay, so you've heard my piece," Bolan said. "What's it going to be?"

"I need to check this with El Jefe."

"Well, you can do that. But don't be surprised if in the next half hour or so this guy pokes his head up at Love Row and starts blowing everything you own to hell and back."

Camano tried to look amused, but the manner of his laugh told Bolan he'd made the MS-13 boss nervous. "Okay, so I've heard about you, and I know El Jefe uses outside help at times. Were you sent here to do me next?"

"Not if you let me do the job I was sent to do."

Camano looked at Flip. "What do you think?"

Flip scratched his neck nervously, keeping his eyes on Bolan. In a quiet voice, he replied, "I think he's legit, *jefe*. His story's too wild to be made up. I, too, have heard of his work for La Salvatrucha and Le Gango Jefe. I think we ought to give him a shot."

"Okay," Camano said. "What did you have in mind?"

"You got ants in and around Love Row?" Bolan inquired, already knowing the answer.

Camano nodded.

"You send them there and we'll meet up, as many as you can spare. We can wait for this Fed. You can send Flip here along if you don't trust me, or at least until you check out my story with your boss. And when you talk to him, you tell him the job's done with Guerra."

"You tell him, *vato*. I ain't no kitchen boy." Camano turned his attention to Flip. "You take two others and go with him. Once you get downtown, give him his piece back. His wheels stay here for now."

"*Sí, jefe.*" Flip turned and waved Bolan toward the door, falling into step behind him as they left.

Bolan remained cool and collected. Through his own ego, Camano had just signed the death warrants of the better part of his force. The numbers would be high and the battle fierce, but at least Bolan would be able to confine the bloodletting to the enemy's ranks. Before the sun set in East Los Angeles, Bolan would deliver a message of death. He had identified the target and isolated it.

Now only one mission objective remained—total destruction!

IN THE AFTERMATH of his enemy's campaign in Herndon, as the fires of urban warfare died, Andries Blood considered his opponent.

He could not help but have great respect for the man. Regardless of whether he was from BATF, Delta Force or some other covert government agency, this Matt Cooper had demonstrated his methodical approach to accomplishing mission objectives. Only a true soldier would operate in such a fashion. Cooper knew his targets. He knew how to identify their weaknesses and exploit them, and he also knew how to plan and execute an operation down to the minutest details. Most of all, he knew the key to success was knowing his enemies, which is why Blood had decided to wait rather than intervene as Cooper wreaked wanton destruction on his client's operations.

Most important, Blood had learned from his observations.

Whatever else this man might be, a consummate warrior and operator aside, he had a weakness—bystanders. Blood had noted his enemy's penchant for avoiding implementation of any operation where civilians might become casualties.

Blood would turn that into Cooper's undoing. He had almost considered taking the warrior at the industrial park on the edge of town, when it was only the Herndon police chief and him, but Blood didn't think it wise to engage his enemy without a foolproof plan.

Instead, Blood waited and followed Cooper from his hit on the gangbangers' den to the industrial park, and eventually the airport, maintaining a cautious vigil to avoid detection. Blood believed he'd pulled it off successfully and now he was glad he'd waited. A couple thousand dollars bought him the information he needed on the destination of the private plane on which his enemy left Dulles the previous night—another thousand bought a one-way ticket to LAX first class.

Blood waited patiently most of the morning, but the plane never arrived. He gave the tail number to an air traffic coordinator, who wasn't cooperative at first, but with some proper incentive—involving the deft use of a knife and cigarette lighter—it hadn't been long before Blood learned of the plane's diversion to a small airport on the outskirts of the city. With the information in hand, Andries Blood eventually tracked Cooper's plane to its true destination and observed through binoculars from an overlook that provided an impressive view of the entire airfield.

For a long time he saw nothing.

But then a sedan showed up and three occupants emerged, Cooper accompanied by a young woman and small child. A mother and daughter, perhaps, or even his enemy's young maiden complete with offspring? Whatever the case, Blood found it interesting that the couple departed again within the hour sans the little girl.

Blood had considered his options.

He knew Cooper didn't suspect he was being followed, otherwise he wouldn't have risked exposing innocents. Blood also figured Cooper had something up his sleeve where it concerned MS-13 operations in Los Angeles. Blood went through his mental records and considered Cooper's motives up until now. Guerra had been one of several shot-callers Marciano's people locked up. There was another in Denver, one in Miami, and then two more here in L.A. One of them was a small-time hood, one who hardly did enough business to be worth the effort.

That left Charles Camano. Blood accessed his PDA and looked up Camano's name inside a database frequently utilized by large private investigative agencies. The site contained an information portal tied into the NCIC system, along with several other major law-enforcement databases. Ah, the power of the information age. It didn't take long for Blood to find Camano's records. Yes, the guy was just the kind of scum that would appeal to his client. At least Cristobal's taste in puppets remained consistent.

Blood memorized the last-known address on file for Cristobal, and a quick look at an online map rendered directions. From here it would take him about a half hour to get to Camano's place. He needed to warn the guy of Cooper's presence here and the trouble it signaled. He started the engine of his rental and headed down the long, gravel road that led from the small promontory. But in his haste to get on with his mission, he missed the red-and-white taxicab that pulled into the airfield less than a minute later.

A cab occupied by a lone woman.

THE WOMAN JUMPED from the cab as she tossed a fifty-dollar bill at the cabbie, who shouted at her she'd forgotten her twenty-something in change. He shrugged and peeled away before either the crazy chick realized her error or decided she actually cared.

Missy rushed to the plane and beat incessantly on the door until Grimaldi came and folded it downward into the stairwell.

"Easy, girl, this is only aircraft aluminum." He noticed the panicked look on her face. "What's wrong?"

"Mike's in trouble," she said. "*Serious* trouble."

Grimaldi chuckled. "He's always in trouble. It's his lot in life."

"You're taking this awfully well."

"I've been through it a few times," Grimaldi deadpanned. As he stepped back to allow Missy to climb the steps and duck inside, she said, "Well, I don't see this is time to make jokes. If it's all the same to you, I've done my part. Now I'm taking my sister and getting out of here." She looked at the girl who was busily coloring in one of her books. "Get your stuff together, sweetie, we're leaving."

"Whoa, hold up there, lady," Grimaldi said. "What's the rush?"

"Chico Camano, that's what." She looked at Grimaldi, tension evident in eyes that took on an aquamarine cast in the soft lights of the plane. "Your friend's gotten himself into some serious shit, and I don't think he'll be coming out any time soon."

"Tell me what happened."

"Uh-uh, I already said I'm done. Now I'm leaving." She turned to notice her sister was still doodling, her tongue protruding between her dainty pink lips in concentration. "I said let's *go,* Samantha. Now!"

"Just take it easy," Grimaldi said, raising his hands. "Please tell me what happened. Where's the Sarge?"

"The *Sarge?*" She snickered. "Are you kidding me?"

"Look, Missy, you want to go then I won't stop you," Grimaldi said in a steady but firm tone. "But that man you left out there puts his neck on the line every minute of every day to help out people just like you. Maybe where you come from abandoning your friends is the status quo, but that isn't the way we do things here. Now if you know where he is and what's going on, you need to tell me because you're not leaving until you do."

Missy looked at him. While remaining calm, Grimaldi had expressed his resolve in a way that removed any doubt on her part that he'd carry through with his promise without reservations. The ace pilot knew it might not have been exactly the way Bolan would have wanted him to handle it, but right at that moment he didn't give a damn. His friend was in trouble and he planned to do whatever he could to help out, and if that meant strong-arming this young lady in front of her little sister, then that's what it meant.

"I don't know what he has planned," she said. "We never got a chance to be alone once we got to Chico's. I'll give you the address to his place."

"That's all you know?" Grimaldi asked.

"That's it. Oh, other than that when we were driving there I do remember him saying he would try to lure Chico's ants into Love Row. I believe he said something about one shot, one kill."

Grimaldi nodded in full understanding now. He'd spent enough time with the Executioner to know exactly how his friend thought, and it made perfect sense. Bolan would be looking to get them clustered into as tight an area as possible, affording him not only a maximum effect but severely minimizing any risk to civilian or law-enforcement casualties. And he would be expecting Grimaldi's support in the effort. It was a plan they had discussed before Bolan went off on his first probe, the one that brought him into contact with Missy and Samantha.

The pilot turned and stabbed a button on the nearby communications panel near the terminal screens as he picked up the blue, wireless phone next to it. There were a few clicks and then Aaron "the Bear" Kurtzman's voice came on the line.

"Bear, it's Eagle. Striker's in hot and I need a chopper, military grade, with full clearance over the area called Love Row. Pronto!"

"Understood. Should be able to deliver to your AO in about twenty minutes."

"Acknowledge. Out here."

Grimaldi hung up the phone. "Listen to me, Missy. I've already told you you're not a prisoner here, so you're welcome to go any time you want. You'll be safe if you decide to wait here, but whatever happens I know the Sarge would want to see you make the best life you can for yourself. So promise me that you'll get as far from here as you can."

Missy nodded and something cracked in her normally tough, haughty expression. Grimaldi couldn't help but notice the glisten of tears starting to form in her eyes. "I'm sorry I couldn't do more for him. And I appreciate everything you guys have done for me, I really do. I won't ever be able to repay you. But the fact is, I'm just not up to this. Can you understand that?"

Grimaldi nodded and replied softly, "Yeah, I can understand it. And so will the Sarge."

As Grimaldi headed toward the cockpit of the plane, Missy said, "Will you be able to help him?"

The Stony Man flier turned, favored her with a cocksure grin and winked. "It's what I was born to do, ma'am."

15

The numbers were running down.

Bolan figured he had less than twelve hours before the facts surfaced and his ruse unraveled at the seams. In fact, he wondered if it would even take that long. At least things had gone as planned so far. He doubted very much anything he had said had convinced Camano to send his crew of ants to Love Row—this was more the MS-13 boss letting his curiosity get the better of him. If it worked, then Bolan wasn't about to look a gift horse in the mouth.

The only task remaining now, and the toughest one of all, would be to get away from his escort. Neither Flip nor his men looked like they would let Bolan off his short leash easily. That meant the warrior would have to fashion a faux encounter with the mysterious government guy, and a crude one at best, to put them on the defensive and make them respond as if they were up against a real enemy.

The plan to do that consisted of two main parts. The first had already been set in motion, thanks to Missy's brilliant performance. They had dropped her back at Love Row, at which point the Executioner surmised she would have acquired transportation and immediately headed for the airport. He'd dropped subtle clues to her in their conversation, and he was banking on the fact she would relate those to Grimaldi in turn. The ace flier would know what to do from there, and if Bolan hedged his bets he knew it wouldn't be long before Grimaldi showed up in a blaze of glory.

The second part had been trickier to foresee but no less important to the plan. When they were still at the airfield, Bolan had rigged the underside of his vehicle with a timer attached to a remote detonator and about six pounds of C-4—enough plastique explosive to blow the vehicle sky high. He'd counted on being able to use the remote and detonate or defuse the charge to meet potential variables in the situation, but he hadn't planned on Camano ordering the vehicle to remain in his custody until everything had panned out.

Still, Bolan's efforts would go a long way toward positioning him in just the right fashion to see the operation through to completion.

Bolan glanced at his watch and noted the time, then looked out the windshield from his place in the backseat of the Crown Victoria wedged between two of Camano's ants. They were big men, and they held the submachine guns in their laps with total indifference. Bolan knew from their casual manner that they wouldn't hesitate to turn those weapons on anyone who got in their way. He marked that for future reference, hopeful he could pull them down before the police or innocents strayed into the line of fire.

Bolan thought for a minute about possible variances as the wheelman turned onto Love Row and drove purposefully for a couple of blocks. Eventually he pulled the vehicle to the curb, and they all climbed from the interior into the noonday heat. The sun now stood high in the sky, which meant Grimaldi would face a few challenges when he arrived with air support.

The Executioner looked up and down the street, watching for pedestrians, but it was just as deserted now as it had been early that morning. It seemed almost surreal to him that just a few blocks away were scores of pedestrian and vehicle traffic; yet, it was like a ghost town here, as if the place had been abandoned for generations. Bolan figured the police patrols in this section probably didn't pick up until nightfall. At least he could be grateful for that much.

The men proceeded inside the club, at which point Flip turned and handed Bolan's pistol to him, butt first. The Executioner took it with a curt nod and immediately tucked it into the holster he wore. The vestibule of the club was dark and cool, the hum of distant air conditioning units the only thing that broke the silence. It reminded Bolan of stepping from the desert into some ancient Egyptian tomb. He tried to let his eyes adjust, but the men pushed him deeper into the club. The sound of footfalls padding away from them echoed in his ears and then a moment later a bath of recessed lights followed the clack of switches being thrown.

The club seemed no less eerie for the lights, although "posh" happened to be the first word that came to Bolan's mind. The floors were made of composite laminate dyed to look like cherrywood, durable for foot traffic and dancing, and the tables were small and spaced adequately. Four chairs with leather seats and velour back pads encircled each of the tables, which were adorned with white linen tablecloths. Bolan recalled Missy's description about working these kinds of places on the escort side, and he could understand why she saw this as a benefit. Obviously this place was reserved for only the richest clientele. Bolan had noted a sign upon entering that stated in no uncertain terms a $50 cover charge and two-drink minimum per head.

"Nice place," the Executioner remarked.

Flip afforded him a wry expression. "Mr. Camano has good taste."

"Where's the rest of the crew?"

"They'll be here soon enough." He waved toward one of the tables. "Sit down and make yourself at home."

Bolan shrugged and sat, his eyes flicking irregularly toward his watch. It would take Grimaldi a half hour at most to arrange transportation. If he calculated the amount of time it took for them to return Missy to this location, then for her to catch a cab to the airfield and make contact with his friend, it wouldn't be long now. With luck, Camano's ants would show up before the Stony Man pilot did.

Fortune or something more had to have favored the Executioner, because it wasn't long before he heard the slamming of car doors. Seconds elapsed, and then it seemed like a small army of men came through the front doors. Bolan estimated twenty-five to thirty guns before he finally stopped counting. It looked like Camano had taken the bait.

Now all he had to do was wait for the fireworks to begin.

ANDRIES BLOOD TURNED onto Camano's street and drove until he reached the hood's estate. He thought about pulling into the driveway but decided to go around the block and make his entry to the grounds without arousing whatever security team Camano might have. Blood had no reason to believe Cooper had even started his campaign against Camano. In fact, the possibility existed that Camano knew Cooper was in L.A. and had sent his men to hunt the man down.

It was possible, Blood thought, but not likely.

Cooper didn't seem to operate that way. He would watch and wait on his enemy, study their movements before devising a battle plan. A cunning warrior, indeed, which made him worthy of Blood's attentions. But they were not equals. Blood knew that whatever happened, Cooper would maintain his motherly pandering to civilians—Blood had no such demons. He would avoid combat scenarios with civilians whenever possible because he was a professional, and because they added less than predictive elements to the field of battle, but he had no qualms about culling a general populace if it meant achieving his objectives.

As Blood parked his car at the curb and exited the vehicle, he wondered for a short time if that might be a simple way of drawing Cooper into a snare. With methodical planning, he could select a body of civilians to endanger and bring Cooper running like a frightened child into its mother's arms. That would make for a reasonable alternate plan, but for now he needed to focus on the advantages to be gained from sticking close to Camano. If necessary, he would use the crime lord as bait.

Blood sauntered casually up the slight rise of the property on the back side of Camano's until he came to a vine-covered fence. Without hesitation, he found hand- and footholds and scaled the eight-foot latticework without trouble, dropping to the other side undetected. He scanned the property in search of electronic detection devices but didn't note any. Cameras were mounted on the corner posts of the patio, but they were pointed toward the house.

Blood waited and observed for a few minutes to ensure no roving guards suddenly showed up, and then he sprinted from his crouched position and made the house unmolested. He was careful to enter from the side, keeping out of the range of cameras as much as possible. He tested the sliding door and found it unsecured. He tugged it slightly, ready to make an exit if an alarm sounded, but the door gave easily and Blood shook his head with disgust. If this was Charles Camano's idea of security, the guy didn't have a clue.

Blood slipped inside and shut the door behind him.

Only silence greeted his ears. It seemed too quiet, really, and Blood had the fleeting sense something wasn't right. Maybe security was lax, okay, but he saw no reason why activities inside the house shouldn't be normal. There were only two reasons for it to be this quiet—either the house was unoccupied or he'd been detected and they were lying in wait for him. Blood inched along the hallway, back to the wall, the neoprene soles of his shoes silent on the hardwood flooring. He reached the other end of the hallway and peered through an open archway into what appeared to be a living area.

Blood turned his attention to the closed door on the other side of the hallway. He reached down and tested the handle, which turned smoothly and silently. He opened the door a crack and peered inside. The interior lights were off, but sunlight filtering through the shears illuminated enough for Blood to make out the details of some kind of office. He opened the door more until he could slip inside, closing it behind him. He crouched and listened but heard no sounds. Maybe Camano was out and the house *was* empty. But then...

Voices. It sounded as if they were coming from outside. Blood moved to the windows of the office and parted the sheers just enough to see out. Several men stood in the circular drive in front of the house, clustered around the open trunk of a car. Something flashed in the back of Blood's psyche, some attempt to recall a fading detail, and then it hit him. He'd seen that car before. It was the one Cooper had been driving. The one he spotted at the airport with the woman and girl!

But what the hell was it doing here?

Blood never had time to concoct a hypothesis in reply to his self-rhetoric because a bright flash—followed by whooshing flames and a powerful shock wave—lodged glass shards in his face and knocked him to the ground. The heat from the explosion combusted the sheers and charred the edges of the window frame. Blood reached toward his head in reflex but quickly pulled his hand away along with blood, glass fragments and some burned skin. It felt like someone had rubbed his face with a sheet of fiberglass, and he instantly knew that he'd suffered serious injuries.

Maybe not fatal, but serious.

Blood shook his head and screamed in agony. He rode the wave of nausea, vomited and then realized it was only due to initial shock. Slowly, painfully, he scrambled to his feet. His right eye felt swollen shut, but he could see out of his left and that would be enough to facilitate his escape. Blood ripped the door open with nearly enough force to detach it from its hinges and staggered down the hallway. As the pain subsided a bit, he licked his lips and tasted blood. He could feel a steady stream running down over his useless right eye, which felt wedged closed whenever he attempted to open it.

Blood wanted to touch his face, scratch at it, but he knew the futility in that and willed his hands to remain at his sides. He had made it off the back patio before he heard shouts behind him. He didn't even bother to look, opting to break into a full sprint for the back fence. Blood crossed the expansive lawn in under ten seconds flat and went up and over the fence without even slowing. He landed hard on the other side, producing a muffled yelp as the impact sent new ripples of pain lancing through his face. Blood pushed the injuries from his mind and sprinted toward his car.

He would have to find a hospital or urgent care facility quickly—there was no way any battlefield medical care would suffice. As he eased his body behind the wheel and started the engine of his car, he had already begun to formulate the story he would tell the doctors and nurses. A welding accident sounded plausible. Maybe a tank exploded and he had been standing behind a window and that's how it happened. With luck, they would buy the story with minimal questions.

Blood knew he was a survivor, if nothing else. And he also knew that Cooper had set him up somehow. But how? He would get those answers soon, but for now he had to attend to his own needs. Later, he would attend to Cooper—and this time he'd finish him.

IGNACIO PAZ COULDN'T be sure how it had happened but somehow when he came out with guns blazing he didn't hit even one of his enemies. Instead, they had caught him off guard and nearly knocked him out cold before dragging his semiconscious form to a nearby vehicle. They roughly bound his hands and feet in hog-tie fashion before tossing him into the backseat of an idling car. His chin struck the opposing armrest of the door and caused him to bite his lip, but Paz held his tongue. He didn't know if he had actually passed out during any point in the trip, but he had to have blacked out for a time because he didn't remember the vehicle actually stopping or being pulled from it.

The next thing he remembered was being dragged downhill on a rough pathway that seemed to darken and cool the deeper it went. Eventually, his captors brought him to an unmarked door that looked like it was made of bamboo cinched tightly together with thick, steel braids. One man opened the door and a second tossed him through it. His hands and feet still tied behind him, he landed on his belly. The wind was knocked from him and he got a mouthful of warm, watery mud. The door slammed shut behind him a minute later.

Paz managed to roll on his side in the mud puddle and spent the better part of the next five minutes spitting the foul dirt from his mouth. The odor of stagnant jungle growth and humid air assaulted his nostrils. And another smell tucked in the recesses of his mind. Death. The average person didn't realize it but death actually had a smell to it, unlike any other. Paz had inspected plenty of bodies during his time with BATF—victims of the gunrunning and illegal import trades—

and each of them had the exact same smell. It was a smell that couldn't be covered up by the chemicals of the morgue or even the mortician's embalming processes. Death was death and it had a smell, and Paz would never be convinced otherwise.

Hell, for all he knew there was a body rotting in a cell next to his. He looked over his head and noticed that the roof was actually a natural canopy of jungle flora, that his prison didn't have a man-made covering. Had he been unbound it wouldn't have proved difficult to get out, so Paz immediately began to work at getting his hands untied. He worked at his bonds for a while, but eventually the rough surface of whatever they had used to bind him began to chafe his wrists to the point that the skin cracked and bled.

Paz finally quit struggling against the ropes and considered alternatives. Yeah, right—like he really had any of those. He took solace in the fact that Mariana had gotten away safely with the children. At least, he *hoped* she had. He couldn't be certain but it seemed only logical that Cristobal had nothing to gain by wasting resources chasing after an impoverished, defenseless woman and her children.

Paz wasn't sure how much time had passed, but suddenly the door flew open and two men stepped in and hauled him off the jungle floor. His shirt clung to his body, wet with mud and coupled with the sheen of sweat that had built up on his skin. The cool air outside, shaded by all of the overhead foliage, bit at his soaked skin but he ignored it. He would need all of his strength and focus for whatever lay ahead of him. Paz had little reason to doubt his captors worked for Cristobal.

Who else would take such an interest in him?

Well, at least now he'd finally managed to penetrate El Gango Jefe's secret headquarters, something that eight months of undercover work hadn't been able to accomplish.

How much money had he spent in bribes?

How many drinks had he bought to loosen lips?

How much time had he spent looking over his shoulder and risking his neck?

And for what? This was what it had required. Do something to draw attention to himself so he could get captured and be brought like a lamb into the lion's den. Paz considered the irony of it all and tried to ignore the ache in his shoulders and ankles as the pair of gorillas literally carried him, bound, up the hill and through a swing screen door that led onto a covered patio. They continued through the deck into the house, and Paz began to draw a chill from the air-conditioned interior.

The men eventually brought him to a wide room with a large mat of plastic beads strewn across a wooden floor. The only other objects in the room were a bar against one wall and a massive wicker chair positioned in front of the mat. A ceiling fan made from what appeared to be bamboo turned lazily above the chair, which was manned on either side by two guards dressed in black slacks and T-shirts, with biceps bulging. The pair wore sunglasses, and neither seemed to even notice Paz was there as his captors tossed him on the hard plastic with the same equal abandon as they had when depositing him in the prison cell.

Paz looked up at the sound of a door opening. A huge, roly-poly looking man entered, wearing a flower-print shirt and loose-fitting pants with a rope tie as a belt. He moved like a slug, and his breathing was labored, probably due to the effort of moving such mass. When he finally sat, the wicker chair creaked loudly, angrily.

"Well," the man said. He held up a torpedo-like marijuana joint and one of the bodyguards leaned forward at the cue and lit it. He took several deep breaths and then held the joint out for one of the men. "Offer some to our friend here. After all, he is our guest."

The muscle man held the doobie in front of Paz's face, but the BATF agent just looked the guy in the eyes with the thought of murder in his heart. The bodyguard grinned before handing it back to his boss. Paz remained silent even though he had about a half dozen questions he was dying to ask the fat slug who sat smoking and grinning before him.

"I've gone to considerable trouble to find out who you are," he said. "I'm still not sure. What I do know is that you have ties to that prick back in Herndon—Gary Marciano."

The sensation he'd swallowed a large marble that settled in the pit of his stomach struck Paz like a lightning bolt, but he kept his expression passive and replied, "Never heard of him."

The fat man cackled. "Sure you haven't. Just like I suppose you don't know who I am."

"I don't."

"My name is Serafin Cristobal," he said. "And in addition to what I've already told you, I know you've been inquiring about me to anybody who will listen. Unfortunately, you picked the wrong friends."

Before Paz could say another word, Cristobal snapped his fingers and the door opened once more.

This time, to admit Mariana.

16

He could hardly believe his eyes. At first he had assumed she was a prisoner, but the truth quickly became apparent when she shuffled over to Cristobal and laid a delicate hand on his shoulder, one which he covered with his own meaty fist.

"Do you know how long I've waited to see that look on your face?" Cristobal inquired.

The entire room burst into laughter. Raucous, mocking laughter that grated on Paz's nerves and sounded like nothing more than broken glass in his ears. He could hardly believe it! Mariana? How could this sweet, innocent girl have allowed herself to be taken in by a piece of shit like Cristobal?

Paz's voice was barely above a whisper and dripped with hatred. "I sometimes have to wonder if there's any place left in all of this stinking country you don't have your maggoty fingers into."

"Nobody talks to me like that!" Cristobal shouted, leaning forward in his seat and gesturing at the bodyguard.

The man who had a minute earlier bent over to offer him drugs now bent to bury a fist in Paz's kidney. Pain shot all the way from his back to a point behind his testicles, and bile formed in his throat. That pain wasn't as bad as when the second blow came, however, and Paz had to wonder if that second one might not have actually burst the tender organ. At best, he could expect it to be bruised and be pissing blood for a week.

"That's enough, Esteban," Cristobal said. He belched,

adding, "What kind of host would I be if I killed my guest on his very first day with me?"

More raucous laughter that died quickly when Cristobal raised his hand for silence.

Paz didn't look at them for the longest time, the pain so great it was an effort to lift his head. When it had finally transformed from white hot burning to a pulsing throb, Paz looked Mariana in the eyes.

"Why?" he rasped. "Why would you do this to your kids?"

"You talk to me!" Cristobal replied. "Besides, those weren't really her kids. They belonged to some other woman who, eh, let's just say had an unfortunate accident. But I, my nameless friend, I am not such a heartless and unfeeling pig as you might think. No, I took those poor kids under my wing and have been seeing to their care. Mariana, here, she happens to be one of my finer agents. Quite talented, especially in the bedroom. Don't you think?"

Paz made no response other than to sneer. Had he been able to muster the strength and gotten to Cristobal before the body-guards intercepted him, he would have wrapped his fingers around the guy's throat and squeezed until his eyeballs popped from his head. He'd been raised in his Catholic faith never to hate any person, but this man? Yes, this man he hated, and before he died he would make sure the man paid for his sins.

Every damn one of them.

"Esteban, I think you should cut our friend loose," Cristobal suggested. "Help him up, eh?"

The man stepped forward, whipped out a knife and flipped the blade into a locked position with one smooth motion. He cut the bonds without pretext, and Paz screamed as his legs and arms were suddenly loosed under the pressure. He screamed as a new wave of pain ran through his lower back from the earlier blows he had suffered. The brute called

Esteban didn't seem to care as he hauled Paz to his feet with no regard for the pain.

Paz bit down his anger and swallowed his pain. He stood on both feet like a man, gritting his teeth and staring daggers at Cristobal. The gang leader, this grand thug of thugs, simply returned the look with drug-induced amusement. Cristobal took another long drag, closing one eye in response to the smoke that curled up and into it.

In a gust of exhalation he said, "Now, where were we? Ah, yes, I believe you were going to tell me your name."

Paz remained silent.

"No? Okay, then, I guess the conversation has ended before it is started. Esteban, take our friend out back. Start by shooting him in the right hand, then bring him back and let's see if he's in more of a mood to talk."

Esteban started to move, but Paz raised his arms. "Wait, wait! Okay…okay, I'll tell you. Though I don't see any difference since you're going to kill me anyway."

"Yes, but if you are honest and thorough, I will order a quick and relatively painless death," Cristobal replied. He tried to look meek but only succeeded in ridiculous. "As I've already said, I'm not an unfeeling man."

"No, you just thrive on stealing from others, corrupting them to further your own ends," Paz said in a sardonic tone. "What's wrong with that?"

"What is wrong with that? It's good business."

"It's criminal."

"It's free enterprise."

"It's wrong."

Cristobal waved at him. "Ah, you don't believe that any more than I do! I've been watching you, listening to Mariana's reports about you with great interest." He tried to act conspiratorial, putting his fat hand against his fat cheek and adding quietly, "I actually think she likes you."

He took another hit and continued, "You have managed to work down here and evade my people with considerable skill. Of course, it was I who let you do that, hoping you would betray your employer. But you did not. You were careful, *very* careful, and those are admirable qualities. But now, your time is over and it would behoove you to cooperate, help yourself. I might even consider suspending your sentence, offering you a job."

"I don't want any of your kind of mercy," Paz said. "I'd never work for scum like you, Cristobal."

"You know what, you're probably right. This is why we should just discontinue this conversation until you're feeling more cooperative. Esteban?"

This time, Paz didn't resist as the bodyguard and his companion moved forward and grabbed his arms. One on either side, they half dragged him through the door and another room of the house to the area out back. The goon whose name he didn't know forced Paz to his knees and pulled up his arm, while Esteban reached beneath his armpit and withdrew the pistol holstered there. It was now or never—Paz had considered his situation, knew he had only one chance to help himself.

And he took it.

THE CELL PHONE on Flip's belt rang shrilly, demanding his attention. He flipped it open one-handed and put the receiver to his ear. He listened for a moment and then his eyes slowly turned to look at Bolan. A minute later the gangster mumbled a response and snapped the lid closed. From the time he'd first looked at Bolan his eyes never left the Executioner.

"There's trouble at the house," he said. "We think it's the guy you told us about."

Bolan shook his head. "How's Chico?"

"He's okay, but I guess the guy blew up your car and then tried to split. Don't matter, though, we got someone tailing him, and it looks like he might be headed this way," Flip replied.

That last part didn't make a bit of sense to Bolan. The charge had gone off as expected, but there hadn't been anybody there to detonate it. Who would they be chasing? For a moment, the Executioner thought Grimaldi might have opted to head for Camano's house rather than come here, but that didn't make any sense, either. If the ace flier had gone to Camano's, he would have arrived by air, not ground vehicle.

Flip turned to the congregation waiting idly and said, "Six of you stay here, my guys with me, and the rest head for Chico's place. Go!"

The crowd of armed men jumped out of their chairs and scrambled for the club exits. Flip turned and gestured for Bolan and the other guys to follow him, and a small team remained, not moving from their spots. The warrior noted how organized they seemed—Flip didn't even have to assign who would stay. Apparently, each of the ants had their details assigned. That showed foresight and organization, and Bolan had to admit it impressed him, as he'd apparently underestimated their training.

However, none of them was prepared for the brilliant explosion that sounded just outside the club. A cloud of dust followed in the wake of the flame that whooshed through one of the doors, ripping it off its hinges and searing the flesh off several men down to the bone. Rubble, plaster and glass shards rained from the ceiling in the aftermath of the shock wave. Bolan reacted with incredible speed and shoulder rolled behind cover even as he suspected a second explosion would follow in short order.

"Damn, that bastard's already here!" he heard Flip shout just before a second explosion blew down more doors and filled the vestibule with thicker billows of dust and black smoke.

Bolan reached the area behind the massive bar on the far side of the club undetected, and then ran in a crouch as he headed for the back kitchen area where he knew he would find a service exit. Nobody within the group seemed interested in him at the moment. Getting under some type of cover and preparing for an enemy that might come through the front entrance was their main concern. This afforded the Executioner ample time to get clear and arrange a rendezvous with none other than that inimitable Grimaldi.

Bolan found the service-entrance door and kicked it open. He stepped into the alleyway and ran toward the front of the building where he knew Grimaldi would be waiting. He could hear the blades of a chopper whipping the air and the droning buzz of turbine engines as Grimaldi hovered over the site and waited for a sign of Bolan. The soldier didn't disappoint him—he burst onto the street and waved his arms. The pilot spotted him immediately and turned the chopper toward an open area two blocks down. Bolan moved as fast as his legs would carry him.

When the Executioner reached the chopper—an MH-60K SOF Black Hawk—he jumped aboard. Grimaldi looked back and Bolan gave him a thumbs-up as he slid into one of the safety harnesses. He then donned a headset and the pilot took the chopper off the ground even as a number of dazed survivors reassembled and took up firing positions to try to shoot down the chopper.

Bolan took up a position behind the M-60 E-4 machine gun free-mounted in the doorway of the chopper. This latest variant, aka the Mk. 43 Mod 0/1, sported Picatinny rails integrated into the feed cover and a proved continuous-fire endurance capability of 850 rounds. While the weapon was a primary service use squad small arms for special operatives of the U.S. Navy, primarily the SEALs, Grimaldi had apparently pulled strings to get an Army chopper equipped with it. In any case, it proved to be most effective against their MS-13 aggressors.

Camano's ants split like a colony exposed to a flamethrower as Bolan triggered his first volley. Brass and belt casings chugged from the extractor as the Executioner rained a merciless hailstorm of 7.62 mm fire on the heads of his enemies. The heavy-caliber rounds ripped through the men. Most of them dropped instantly as the rounds punched through vital organs, and a couple even took volleys to the head, their skulls exploding under the pressure effects of the slugs. In some cases, the damage was nearly severe enough to all but decapitate the MS-13 gunners.

Bolan eased off the trigger as Grimaldi flew out of range, turned the chopper and then headed back the way they had come to afford him another chance to buzz their opponents. The Executioner poured an unending stream of autofire with the kind of deadly accuracy that had earned him his moniker. When flesh-and-blood opportunities weren't present, Bolan took a moment to redecorate the facade of the club.

Dust and smoke rose from the front of the club as the stench of heat and battle assailed Bolan's nostrils. Even at that position he could tell they had dealt a crippling blow to the enemy. Bolan keyed up the headset and ordered Grimaldi to pull back.

"What's up?" the pilot asked once they were clear.

"I want to hold position and wait for them to leave," Bolan replied. "You got most of them with that first missile attack. Your timing was impeccable."

"Read your mind, did I?"

"That you did, Ace. That you did."

"Where are you looking to follow the stragglers?"

"One of Camano's chief goons told me they were following somebody who fled the guy's house right after my little present went off in the drive," Bolan replied. "Guess they're blaming whoever it is for that rather than me. I'm interested to know who they're following."

"And you think Camano's people will lead you to him and the remainder of his force," Grimaldi concluded.

"Right," Bolan said.

They didn't have to wait long. True to the Executioner's words, Flip showed up out front a minute later and jogged down the street with survivors from his entourage. Bolan watched through the long-distance range finder, Grimaldi having taken the Black Hawk far enough out that Flip and his boys wouldn't know they were being observed. Just after they jumped in their vehicles and rushed from Love Row, the first of the police units and other emergency vehicles began to arrive.

Bolan nodded with satisfaction—Los Angeles's finest would be able to mop up what little remained.

Grimaldi expertly guided the chopper onto a course of covert pursuit. Bolan couldn't be sure where they would go, but he hoped whoever Camano's boys were chasing that it would lead them away from populated areas. He continued monitoring Flip's vehicle through the advanced, long-range targeting system. Bolan had folded in the weaponry and closed the doors so as to minimize the forces of wind shear and make Grimaldi's piloting efforts easier. Eventually, their quarry grabbed the I-10/San Bernardino Freeway headed east. They continued out of the city and through the suburbs, the traffic relatively light this time of the day—at least compared to rush hour.

The chase continued through West Covina and additional suburbs like Ontario. Bolan began to wonder just how far they were headed, since they had now advanced far beyond Camano's neighborhood. It then thinned out and gave them considerably more open ground. The crew's vehicle slowed, and Bolan spotted some additional vehicles directly ahead of their quarry, clustered in pursuit of a plain sedan. Bolan leaned forward and tapped Grimaldi on the shoulder. The pilot looked over at his friend long enough to see the Executioner point it out, and then increased speed and banked the chopper into position for the intercept.

Bolan readied himself for the fight. This was it, the moment he'd been waiting for. It was time to put Charles Camano and his MS-13 hoods out of business once and for all. With any luck, the prey they were after would be on his side. But if not, he was prepared to do whatever was necessary to see that things went no further. This day was the accepted day of retribution, and the Executioner planned to deliver it with unbridled fury.

MAYBE IT WAS FATE, maybe just a burning desire to live, but Ignacio Paz somehow managed to overcome the pair of behemoths intending to do him bodily harm.

As the one captor held out his arm, Paz recalled a technique he'd once learned from his martial arts instructor at FLETC—Federal Law Enforcement Training Center. He had remembered being told that every part of their training was important, and that one day something they had been taught might actually save their lives. He hadn't really believed it until this moment. But as he yanked his arm downward to pull the man gripping it and swung his legs out from under him in a scissor-kick fashion to complete the takedown, Paz found a reason to change his mind.

Unsteadied and propelled forward to the point of no return, Cristobal's bodyguard collapsed into Esteban as he was drawing his pistol. The man's skull contacted Esteban in the groin and caused him to drop his pistol. The weapon bounced and skittered across the ground, coming to a stop inches from Paz's fingertips. He ignored the pain as he stretched out to scoop the weapon into his hand and point it straight at Esteban. He squeezed the trigger once and at the same moment let out a blood-curdling scream. It would do no good to attempt escape if his captors realized he'd overpowered Cristobal's men. The charade had to play out, at least to afford him enough time to slip into the jungle.

Paz was on the second bodyguard before he could recover. He snaked a forearm around the man's neck and dug a knee into his back while applying a modified rear naked chokehold as he'd been taught in the Marine Corps. Paz strained every muscle in his body, palms clasped together, digging his knee so deeply into the man's back he could actually feel the popping of vertebrae as they shifted. It took less than a minute to render the man unconscious.

Paz thought about maintaining pressure but realized the seconds were ticking and to stay behind and kill the guy would lessen his chances for a clean escape. Sooner or later Cristobal would send someone to investigate why Esteban and his partner had not returned with one BATF agent sporting a bullet hole through his right hand, bleeding and begging for mercy. Paz jumped to his feet, pistol in hand, and crashed into the dense jungle beyond. Stealth and subterfuge were no longer the orders of the day. He needed to make contact with anyone back in the States and get help.

It was time to get the hell out of El Salvador and back home where he belonged. And he knew he'd have to do it on his own—there wouldn't be any white knight riding in on a fiery steed to pull his bacon out of the fire. He was alone, poorly armed and injured, to what extent he didn't know. But the spirit to complete his duty lay deeper within him, a fire burning hotter than those kindled by the thought of any torture or death Cristobal might be able to conjure up in his sick, twisted mind. If he got the chance, though, he would kill that bastard.

Even if it was the last thing he did.

THE CHASE CONTINUED east on I-10 until the lone driver in the sedan got off at Interstate 15 and headed north. The traffic had now thinned considerably, and Bolan could see approximately a half-dozen vehicles were actually in pursuit. The Executioner couldn't be sure if Camano was in one of them, but whatever the case he knew it would soon be time to act. The only way to get clear would be putting the attention of Camano's boys on something other than the sedan they were pursuing.

"If we're going to make our move, we'd better do it now," he told Grimaldi.

The pilot nodded and decreased speed until he was keeping pace with the cluster of chase cars below. Bolan opened the side door of the chopper and put the M-60 E-4 machine gun into battery. He locked it into a forward position on the mounts, targeted the tires of one of the chase vehicles and triggered several volleys. Sparks ricocheted off the pavement as Bolan fired short bursts to find his range. Finally, the last volley had the intended effect of taking out the wheels of two chase vehicles. At those speeds, they were quick to lose control.

The first vehicle spun out and was T-boned by the one immediately behind it before either driver could do anything about it. A third reacted admirably but overcorrected his skid and slid off the road. The vehicle rode up onto a guardrail and continued for about fifty feet until it contacted one of the concrete stanchions holding the rail in place. The vehicle flipped up and over the rail and dropped roof-first into a ravine, crashing into approximately four feet of brackish water.

With three out of six of Camano's vehicles out of commission, the odds had been narrowed tremendously. The driver of the sedan had apparently seen the activity, because the vehicle swerved toward an exit less than a minute later, one that led to a virtually abandoned road. The quarry didn't even slow, blowing the intersection light as he turned right at the bottom of the exit ramp and poured on the speed. Camano's three vehicles followed, apparently intent on catching their guy at any cost.

Grimaldi followed suit by speeding ahead of the caravan of four vehicles and proceeding a couple of miles down the road. He looked at Bolan, who threw him a thumbs-down gesture.

"Put us down, Jack," Bolan said.

Grimaldi nodded even as he maneuvered the stick into position and dropped so fast Bolan felt the roll in his stomach. While the pilot got ready to land, Bolan disengaged his safety harness, reached into the chest of equipment the pilot had brought from their plane and withdrew an FNC. He scooped up a few clips, stuffed them into whatever pockets were free and then detached the M-60 E-4 from the mount. Bolan jumped from the chopper and raced across a grassy field that led up to the crest of a small knoll. He hit the peak on his belly, positioned the machine gun and settled into target acquisition on the mob of vehicles headed straight toward his position.

Bolan waited until the lead vehicle passed, then narrowed in on the one immediately behind and opened up with a full salvo. Flame spit from the muzzle of the M-60 E-4, and Bolan could feel the press of heat from the still hot barrel as he delivered a merciless stream of 7.62 mm fire at Camano's crews. The windshield of the first vehicle spiderwebbed and a moment later the car swerved off the road. As it turned away from him, exposing the driver's side, Bolan could see the bloody remains of the lifeless driver. The vehicle bounced along a muddy rut and splashed to a halt, its nose wedged in the tributary that fed the same ravine into which the other vehicle had crashed minutes earlier.

Bolan had already turned his sights on the remaining two vehicles but didn't have to work hard. The roar of a low-flying chopper buzzed over his position, followed by several successive reports that had a whip-crack effect on the Executioner's ears. A moment later those echoes were drowned by the blast effect of the small rockets Grimaldi had launched at one of the remaining pair of vehicles. The vehicle exploded with such force the blasts actually lifted it off the ground while it was in motion. A secondary explosion sheared the roof from it, leaving a flaming hulk to come down on its suspension as the four tires that had held it on the road were melted to black, gooey slag. The Executioner grinned with satisfaction even as he turned the M-60 E-4 on the last vehicle chasing the sedan.

The quarry had now stopped and bailed from his car. His face was beet red, and it looked like maybe he'd suffered some significant injuries, but Bolan couldn't help him until he neutralized the threat. The man ran toward a run-down shack surrounded by tall undergrowth, probably hoping to find cover from a position he could hold for some extended period of time. As the remaining enemy vehicle skidded to a halt behind the escaping man's sedan, Bolan jumped to his feet—discarding the machine gun—and primed the FNC as he trotted down the other side of the knoll.

Bolan looked to his left and watched as Grimaldi, who had turned the chopper around, headed for the final target. The Executioner raised his hand to indicate he was clear and took a knee just as Camano's gunners bailed from their car in pursuit of the lone man. They looked like ravenous wolves chasing after wounded prey, and Bolan felt no remorse as he leveled the FNC and delivered a fusillade of rounds at them.

A couple twisted under the impact of Bolan's unerring accuracy, and the remaining gunners turned, stopped their pursuit and swung their weapons toward Bolan—apparently having forgotten about the air support he commanded. The sky suddenly came alive, like an electric storm, as Grimaldi opened up with a 30 mm chain gun. Scores of rounds cut through the area like angry hornets, chewing apart dirt, metal and flesh with equal ferocity. The pathetic few combatants were no match for that kind of firepower, and by the time Grimaldi eased off the trigger and roared past them not one of Camano's ants remained standing.

The Executioner climbed to his feet and walked purposefully toward the ramshackle structure that had once been someone's home, a home long forgotten with its faded charcoal-gray paneling and collapsing roof. It took him only a few minutes to find the man he'd been searching for. He lay on the ground a few yards from the toppled structure in tall grass, panting and wheezing heavily. His face was almost unrecognizable, filled with glass and scorched in many places. The burns were so severe that much of the skin had blistered or sloughed off to leave the raw flesh of face muscles exposed.

The guy's voice was a rasp as he looked at Bolan. "This... wasn't how it...was supposed to end, Cooper."

Bolan was surprised the man knew his name. "Who are you?" he inquired.

The man could barely respond now. "Not...not important. Only important that...I ad-admit you...have won."

The horror of it suddenly came upon Bolan. The poor helpless man who lay on the ground dying in front of him wasn't a victim of Camano's ruthless underworld activities, neither was he an innocent pawn caught by Bolan's explosives handiwork. This was the real assassin sent by Cristobal, the one who had killed Guerra and—if Bolan had called it correctly—had come to Los Angeles to deliver a similar fate to the Executioner. It was strange how his enemy, a cold and calculating type, had been brought to his demise by a mere act of destiny. He could not have planned this outcome.

Once more Fate had shown its twisted humor and played the cruelest joke of all.

"Kill me…." the guy grated.

But Bolan never had to go that far as the breath the man used to utter that one, simple request for mercy turned out to be his final one. And so a nameless and almost faceless animal, one who had just hours before planned to eliminate the Executioner, surrendered his ghost to an eternal damnation much greater than any Bolan could have conjured in this plane of existence.

17

They were surprised to find Missy and Samantha waiting for them at the plane.

From the way Grimaldi had talked, Bolan got the distinct impression the ex-prostitute and her sister would have been long gone. As the Executioner dropped tiredly down from the chopper, Missy rushed to him and threw her arms around his neck. Bolan couldn't be sure exactly how to take her rather unceremonious greeting, so he settled for giving her a gentle squeeze before disentangling from her to begin the equipment offload.

"I knew you'd come through this alive. I just *knew* it!" More quietly, she added, "I prayed for it."

"I appreciate the vote of confidence," Bolan told her with a grin.

Grimaldi poked his head out and said, "Hey! He couldn't have done it without me."

Missy looked at the pilot awkwardly but then patted his face with her hand. "Okay, I guess kudos are in order for you, too."

"I was kind of hoping for a medal," Grimaldi cracked. "But I guess that'll do."

"I can take care of this," Bolan told the pilot, gesturing at the equipment. "Why don't you get ready to lift off?"

"Right." Grimaldi hopped out of the chopper and headed straight for the plane with purpose in his stride.

Bolan gathered the equipment boxes Grimaldi had brought

from the Gulfstream C-21A, enlisted Missy's help carrying a couple of the lighter ones, and the pair made their way aboard the jet. As Grimaldi completed his preflight check, Bolan busied himself stowing the equipment and then dropped into the chair once he had completed his work. He rubbed his eyes and then yawned and stretched.

The warrior looked over at Missy, but she met his eyes only a moment before looking away. In the receding afternoon light through the windows he caught the slight flush on her cheeks, and Bolan realized she'd been embarrassed by the fact he'd caught her watching him. She pretended to busy herself with Samantha—as if there had been no exchange between them—but Bolan wasn't fooled. He knew about her kind of infatuation because he had dealt with it on many previous occasions. She wasn't in love with him—she was in love with the *idea* of being in love with him.

In a sense, it surprised the Executioner that a woman of her experience didn't act a bit less like a naive schoolgirl and more like the competent, attractive woman he knew she was. Lesser men might have tried to take advantage of her, but nobody could have ever classified Bolan as a lesser man. He no longer saw the prostitute who he'd handed nearly ten thousand in cash—he saw a young and vibrant woman with the guts and brains to make a better life for her and her sister, one that would be filled with satisfaction and security.

In an awkward and eerie moment, almost as if she'd been reading his thoughts, Missy turned and met his wistful gaze. Bolan simply acted as if he didn't even see her looking at him. He had taken as much of a protective interest in Missy and Samantha as she had taken an amorous one in him.

"I just thought you'd like to know," Missy said as the plane taxied onto the runway and Grimaldi prepared to take off. "I appreciate what you did for me—" she stroked some strands of long, blond hair out of Samantha's eyes "—for *us,* I mean. I won't forget it. Ever. And I won't blow this chance. I just thought you should know that."

"I know you won't," Bolan said. He inclined his head toward her sister. "Sam's a pretty lucky little girl she had you around to take care of her after your parents died."

She nodded with a slight smile, an almost reminiscent expression, but then it became a bit harder. Quickly she asked, "You have any sisters?"

Bolan shook his head. "One."

"You ever get to see her?"

"She's dead. Long time ago."

"I'm sorry."

The Executioner gave a sharp nod and put the twinge of pain and regret from his mind. "Thanks."

"Your parents still alive?"

Bolan shook his head, but then on afterthought he added, "I have a brother, but I don't get to see him very much."

"I'd imagine a guy in your line of business wouldn't."

"What do you mean?"

"What you do. If you had any kind of *real* relationship with him, he'd be in danger and you'd have to be in fear of his life all the time, I would suppose."

Missy's forthrightness and insight all at once surprised Bolan and warmed him. In other circumstances, such a woman as this would have proved a great asset to Bolan's activities. It had been a long time since he'd met a woman so deep and compassionate with such a tough and pragmatic exterior. She had rare traits, to be sure, and the Executioner had suddenly acquired a new level of admiration for her.

"You should be a social worker," Bolan said.

This brought a laugh out of her, a nice laugh but a loud one.

"Maybe I could have, but I don't think I'd pass the background check. And could you see me heading up a support group?"

This made Bolan smile. She had a sense of humor, too. No, he'd met a select few like Missy in his travels. She was an odd character, tough but gentle.

"We'll be stopping in Texas to refuel," Bolan said as a change of topic. "I'm afraid that's as far as we can take you."

She nodded. "It works. I've never been there, but I'm sure it'll make for a fresh start."

Bolan nodded and then popped out a recessed shelf in the countertop with the advanced communications equipment and withdrew a card. He wrote a couple of phone numbers down and handed it to her. She took it, looked at what he'd scrawled and then fixed him with an askance expression.

"I owe you big for getting me inside Camano's circle," Bolan said. "You ever have trouble or need anything, you call one of those numbers and ask for a man named Hal. Tell him how you know me, and you can be sure you'll get whatever you need."

She nodded, enfolding the card within her hands, head down. When she finally looked up, the Executioner could see the remnant of tears where they had streaked down her face, leaving glistening trails on her cheeks. "Why are you doing this for me?"

Bolan frowned as he figured out how to tender a measured reply. "Missy, we all make decisions in life sometimes we wish later we hadn't. I know because I've made a few myself over the years. But the only way we can learn to survive while still retaining a bit of our humanity is by turning as many failures as possible into successes. I figure one of my jobs, and I have a lot of them, is to reach out every so often and lend a helping hand. Giving people the benefit of the doubt and believing that they can still change is my way of turning my own failures into success stories."

"Some might call that guilt, Cooper."

"I prefer to call it change," Bolan replied quietly. "You know what I do, the business I'm in. I do what I do out of duty and at the risk of sounding like an egotist, I've learned over the years to sense what's good and what's rotten about most people. I have to believe every now and then that people are capable of changing their lives around and giving back to the betterment of society. I have to help people like you."

"Oh," Missy said with a knowing wink. "We have a man of philosophy here."

"Not philosophy. Facts."

"And what if I don't turn out to be everything you think I can be?"

"It's not about you being what I think you should, it's what *you* think. That's the only important thing. Remember this, if you take nothing else I say with you. The power to change the world for the better starts with exercising the right to change ourselves. You understand that?"

Missy smiled, wiped the residue of tears from her cheeks and said, "I understand."

WHILE THE GOODBYES with Missy and Samantha had been bittersweet, the Executioner knew he couldn't dwell on it. He had one mission objective remaining, and he planned to throw all of his energies into accomplishing that goal. A man's life, namely Ignacio Paz, hung in the balance and time was not a luxury he could afford. As soon as they were airborne and bound for El Salvador, Bolan contacted Stony Man to deliver a report and obtain any additional information they might have for him.

"Nice job in L.A., Striker," Brognola told him. He was sharing space on the split screen of the LCD monitor aboard the Stony Man jet with Price.

"Thanks," Bolan said. "Although I can't confirm I actually got Camano."

"Oh, you got him," Price replied. "It took some doing but we managed to learn just a short time ago his body was identified among those of his numerous MS-13 comrades."

The news should have made the Executioner feel better, but somehow it didn't. "Any word on Paz?"

"Yes, as a matter of fact," Brognola said. "Barb?"

"Paz managed to make contact with a DEA agent working undercover in San Salvador who helped him reach out to his higher-ups at the BATF," Price stated. "He's alive and unharmed, and he fingered Serafin Cristobal at the top of Mara Salvatrucha activities throughout the U.S., as well as about a half-dozen other countries in the Western Hemisphere. Paz was captured and taken to Cristobal's base of operations, but he got away."

"He knows where the headquarters are?"

"Yes, but he's concerned that by the time we get somebody to him they'll have moved their operations."

"Not likely," Bolan said. He looked at a digital clock mounted above the cockpit door that Grimaldi programmed with their ETA. "We'll be touching down in less than five hours."

"Okay, fair enough," Brognola said. "We'll make arrangements for Paz to meet with you."

"What about political considerations?"

"As soon as we heard Paz was alive," Price said, "the President made some calls. The Chief of State has assured him they have no problem looking the other way for twenty-four hours."

"They're not any happier about this deal with Cristobal and MS-13 than we are," Brognola added. "It doesn't make much sense for them politically or financially to refuse help. The military security forces and police have agreed to keep out of sight until you've had a chance to get in there, assess the situation and decide on a course of action. And, of course, they're more than willing to provide backup support should we ask for it."

"The only one who's going to need that is Cristobal."

Brognola grinned from ear to ear. "I figured you might say that."

"I think you should know, Hal, that even when I take Cristobal out of the loop that we'll still have quite a ways to go. It will take time to eliminate the MS-13 threat entirely," Bolan said.

"Understood. But at least we'll be giving our men and women in law enforcement a fair chance by breaking down the superstructure of this little empire Cristobal's managed to carve out for himself."

The Executioner knew his friend spoke the truth, but he also knew that all empires fell eventually—their demise usually caused by the very same factors that had contributed to their rise to power. All of the great emperors of the past, from Augustus to Nero and the early Spanish monarchs up through Napoleon, had been eventually crushed under the weight of their own oppression and greed. Every dog had its day—it was time for someone to inform Serafin Cristobal that his had come and gone.

And Bolan was more than happy to deliver the message.

A HOT, MUGGY WIND brushed Bolan's face as he took survey of the tarmac at the makeshift airstrip on the fringes of San Salvador.

Grimaldi would have landed at the airport in the city but Bolan dissuaded him from it, concerned Cristobal's extensive contacts might learn of their arrival and send scouts to observe their movements. Any chance Bolan had of hitting Cristobal's encampment with any sort of effectiveness would require secrecy right up to the moment of engagement. Bolan didn't think it was wise to advertise that fact beforehand, particularly since the immediate threat to Ignacio Paz's life had been nullified.

A stocky, muscular man in a khaki shirt and shorts waited on the tarmac alongside a second man, this one much taller and well built. They headed toward the plane with caution as the jet engines whined down and Grimaldi killed power to the aircraft. Bolan descended the steps of the plane and awaited their arrival. The taller man extended his hand and on closer inspection Bolan identified him as Ignacio Paz.

"Colonel Stone?" Paz inquired, using the military cover name Stony Man had assigned him.

Bolan nodded. "Good to see you alive, Paz."

"Good to be alive, sir," Paz replied amiably. He gestured to the other man who shook hands with Bolan in turn. "This is Special Agent Quinones with the DEA. *And* my saving angel."

"Pleasure, Colonel," he said. "My people have informed us your reputation precedes you. It's nice to see someone's finally going to shut down this son of a bitch, Cristobal, for good. Guy's a piece of shit…real vermin."

Bolan didn't bother to reply, although he could hardly blame Quinones for his dislike of Cristobal. DEA agents assigned to detachments were notoriously underrated and quite accustomed to working behind the scenes. They were also used to no recognition and no credit for their efforts, since often they had to operate out of the country—oftentimes in complete secrecy—to deter the export of drugs into the United States.

Bolan looked at Paz and asked, "You have a general location of this camp where Cristobal's hiding?"

"I know exactly where it's at," Paz told the Executioner. "I just don't have many details as to its layout or numbers of resistance you may encounter."

Bolan shook his head. "Don't worry about that. I'm banking we'll have surprise on our side."

"Yeah… About that, Colonel. I know you're here to accomplish some specific mission objectives, and I'm willing to let this be your show. All the way." He glanced at Quinones as if looking for moral support, then continued, "But if it's all the same to you, I'd kind of like to be involved. I mean, I owe this bastard for some of things he did to me, and I'd like the chance to pay him back."

"Revenge isn't good business, Ignacio. It clouds reasonability."

"No, no," Paz protested, "I'm not talking about revenge, here. It's just, well, this guy took something from me, and I feel like I need to get it back."

"Your honor," Bolan ventured.

"Yeah, and a lot of other things. Listen, sir, I've spent eight months trying to run this guy and his goons down for Marciano. He took the reward for that effort from me when he had Marciano and Ysidro Perez killed. He has to account for that. I just want to help send him the reminder."

Bolan considered the request, searching Paz's eyes for any hint of fanaticism or deception, but he read only determination and resolve in those intense features. There wouldn't be any putting him off, and the Executioner knew if he denied letting Paz get involved the guy might just go off half-cocked and take matters into his own hands. He couldn't afford that kind of liability. Bolan had enough innocent blood on his hands, and if he had the opportunity to avoid more, then he would take it.

Besides, he could understand where this man was coming from. He'd been a lot like him once.

"All right, Paz," Bolan said. "You're in."

"Could you use some more help?" Quinones ventured.

"You any good with a sniper rifle?" Bolan asked.
"Bear shit in the woods? *Sir?*"
The Executioner nodded. "Then let's get to work."

18

The three Americans walked single file along the dark, verdant jungle trail. The sun had long set beyond a watery horizon, and from the coast a sliver of orange light remained but did not reach them. Even the jungle fauna that normally roamed in the trees above, the macaws and their other less-colorful brothers, had fallen to silence.

Bolan knew the jungle. He'd spent more of his time as a soldier on this kind of terrain than just about any other, except for maybe the urban landscapes of the world's cities. But the jungle was where his body, mind and spirit had been forged into a single entity with one unified purpose: destruction of the enemy.

As they picked their way past the thick trees and tangled creepers, the Executioner had volunteered to take point, and he didn't accept any argument against it—not that Paz or Quinones argued with him. True to Paz's word, they were more than willing to submit to his authority, whether due to his command presence or their sense of his natural leadership abilities. All three men were attired in jungle fatigues and boots. They didn't speak a word as they made their way through the dark, twisted paths carved naturally from the trees and flora. Bolan stopped several times, halting the party with a raised fist and searching the area ahead with eyes and ears attuned to any potential threats. Then he would gesture for them to move again once he'd deemed it safe passage.

By the time they reached their target, any residual light had succumbed to nightfall and silence prevailed.

Paz reached out and touched Bolan's shoulder. The Executioner turned and watched as the man pointed to his eyes and then toward the vast expanse arrayed before them to indicate they had reached their intended destination. Bolan nodded and then ordered Paz and Quinones to spread out in a skirmish line. They had planned their approach on Cristobal's encampment to the minutest detail. Paz had been able to provide at least a partial sketch of the layout, including the main house along with its proximal location to the makeshift cells where they had held him.

When they were in position on the perimeter of the clearing, Bolan silently withdrew a pair of night-vision goggles, raised them to his eyes and studied the terrain. The images were fuzzy, at best, since the light was minimal, but Bolan knew they were in the right spot. He heard the steady hum of a generator, probably buried, and could discern the outline of several structures. Cristobal's security force had done an admirable job in the layout, using as much of the jungle's natural structure to conceal the encampment from prying eyes. Bolan could see two main buildings, one being the house and the other probably a billet positioned opposite it, with an open area separated by a span of perhaps thirty to forty yards.

All three men wore earpieces with throat mics, SEAL-team-style communication Bolan had provided from the essential covert operations equipment stowed aboard the plane. He keyed up the communication link by depressing the button on the face of the throat mic.

"I'm going in," he whispered. "Four minutes and…mark."

The Executioner didn't wait for a reply because he knew there wouldn't be one. It was a fortunate condition of both Paz and Quinones's training in covert operations not to speak unless absolutely necessary, and only then to keep it as brief as possible.

Bolan stored the NVD binoculars and then slid from concealment behind a large fern. He moved silently, remaining hunched as he carefully placed his foot before putting weight down. In addition to the load-bearing harness that sported grenades and a combat knife, along with the Desert Eagle and Beretta 93-R at hand, Bolan clutched his FNC, stock extended and locked against his shoulder, with the muzzle directed wherever he looked. He reached the smaller of the two buildings, the one he guessed to be a bunkhouse of sorts, and crouched near the foundation.

The soldier slung the FNC and then reached into the charges satchel at his hip, withdrawing four quarter-pound sticks of C-4 bundled with electrical tape. A blasting cap with an electronic remote detonator protruded from the puttylike plastique. The warrior had brought three such identical configurations in order to achieve two purposes: provide noise and confusion. Cristobal's people might have been trained, but they weren't likely experienced in the arts of warfare like the Executioner. Such military-grade explosives would not only do considerable damage to structures and equipment within the camp, but it would also bring the enemy running straight into the ambush he'd planned.

Bolan set the charge between the cinder-block foundation and an open-air vent below the base of the billet, and then moved his way around to the other side to plant an additional charge. He stopped and listened, intent on locating the generator. In all likelihood, it would be placed about three to four feet belowground with cans of diesel, or perhaps even a pump-enabled drum. When he pinpointed the probable location, Bolan left his position and moved toward it.

The soldier closed the gap quickly and quietly, but when he got within twenty yards he encountered a sentry. It didn't surprise him. Even Cristobal would have been smart enough to post a roving guard given Paz's recent escape. For all Cristobal knew, Paz might have returned with a small army. In a sense, he'd returned with something far better than that—he'd brought the Executioner.

Bolan took cover at the base of a massive tree and waited until the sentry had gone past. He held his breath, his Ka-Bar fighting knife at the ready, but the sentry didn't spot him and kept on moving. The Executioner's plan depended on creating as much chaos as possible to disorient Cristobal's security force, and he considered the generator a key target. Without power, the enemy would be without communications or lights, unable to call for reinforcements and forced to fight in pitch-black jungle. If Bolan took out the sentry unnecessarily, someone might miss him and generate a camp-wide alert. That would introduce variables for which he hadn't accounted, and the assault would no longer be conducted on *his* terms.

Bolan waited a minute before he rose and continued toward the generator. He eventually located it and then referred to the luminous hands of his watch. Less than a minute to go. The soldier crouched and put his fingers to the ground, searching for where the vibration of the generator was strongest. His fingers settled on something rigid and with a bit of awkward groping he discovered it was a massive piece of plywood concealed beneath dirt, plants and an infrared-resistant tarp. Bolan lifted the board just enough to drop the third charge beneath it, then left the area and headed for the perimeter.

After he'd advanced a safe distance, Bolan unslung his FNC and pulled a long, slender box from one of the pockets of his jungle fatigue shirt. The innocent looking box was the handiwork of Hermann "Gadgets" Schwarz—Able Team's electronics wizard. It was fashioned from a nonconductive composite based on Kevlar material. It was waterproof, durable and contained several switches recessed into it that could remotely trigger up to eight separate charges.

Bolan drew out the antenna with his teeth, took shelter behind a large tree surrounded with heavy brush and keyed the first two charges. The briefest moment of silence reigned followed by a brilliant flash of light. The explosion sent superheated gas into the air, ignited by red-orange flames that easily reached twenty feet in height. Wood shards and splinters that weren't incinerated in the blast rained to the ground in flaming bits. There were shouts combined with screams from personnel obviously caught in the immediate blast area.

Flames whooshed from beneath the air gaps of the plywood boards covering the generator as Bolan detonated the third charge. Only a couple of lights in the house and a spot positioned at one corner of the perimeter had time to come on before the C-4 did its job and rendered blackout mode throughout the entire camp. Gallons of ignited diesel fuel gushed from the crater left by the initial blast and splashed with gooey adherence onto nearby foliage. A couple of sentries who happened to be running past spontaneously flamed into human torches.

Bolan dropped them with mercy rounds from the FNC.

The charges had produced the desired effect. Bolan keyed the throat mic and ordered, *"Now."*

Men scrambling in every direction either dived for cover or tumbled into one another as Paz and Quinones opened up fire simultaneously. Paz had opted for a British-made L86A1 Light Support Weapon manufactured by Enfield Lock. The weapon chambered 5.56 mm NATO rounds and boasted a cyclic fire rate of more than 700 rounds per minute. Bolan had suggested it to the young BATF agent because of its portability, a factor he knew would be important during their travel to the hard site. Round after round pummeled the panicked security force trying to respond to the swiftness and brutality of the Executioner's handiwork.

Quinones had chosen the more traditional M-16 A-2/M-203, given his military training in the U.S. Army's Special Forces. The guy proved his proficiency as he poured on a stream of 5.56 mm lead—not uncontrolled bursts but steady and sustained for maximum effect—with interspersed points of dropping 40 mm HE grenades in spots where the resistance had foolishly clustered together.

Bolan waited for the three minutes as agreed while the two federal cops wreaked havoc on the encampment. When the reports from their weapons finally died out, the soldier scrambled to his feet and rushed inside the perimeter to begin the close-quarter-battle phase of the assault.

The flames that crackled at various points throughout the camp produced enough smoke to cover Bolan's advance, but it also made things a bit more difficult in his search for enemy stragglers. The soldier nearly walked into a pair of MS-13 gunners running pell-mell through the smoke, maybe looking for survivors or possibly just looking to get the hell out of there. He leveled his FNC and triggered a rising, corkscrew burst. The FNC spit flame as Bolan's rounds chewed a swathing pattern through the stomachs and chests of his opponents. He'd already moved on to search for additional targets before either body hit the ground.

The opposing exterior walls of the billets were now awash in flame and the smoke had thickened, becoming blacker as the flames chewed up the timber supports. One man staggered from the front door as Bolan approached and stepped right into the Executioner's path. He was unarmed and trying to rub smoke from his eyes, and the soldier's front-kick to the side caught the man completely by surprise. The force drove him to the ground, and Bolan finished the assault with a boot stomp behind the ear that rendered him unconscious.

The Executioner considered sweeping the interior of the billet for survivors, but the amount of smoke and heat billowing from the front door changed his mind. Anyone else coming out of there would likely be the same as the opponent he'd just neutralized. There were other, more immediate threats with which he needed to contend. Finding Serafin Cristobal was at the top of the list.

Bolan changed direction and headed for the main house. The smoke had started to clear here, and he got to his belly and crawled the remaining distance, lessening the chance that someone positioned at a window might see him and cut him down before he had the chance to respond. Bolan approached the spread until he reached the crude steps that led to the main entrance. He removed the final charge, dropped it beneath the steps and then scrambled clear of the blast area. The soldier skirted around to the side of the house, opened his mouth to prevent the shock from disorienting him and detonated the explosive. Even where he'd sought cover, Bolan could feel the tremors and heat from the blast. Flaming shards erupted in every direction as wooden planks were torn from their metal rivets and sent airborne. Bolan settled into a crouch at the corner and peered around it. Only a smoking hole remained in place of the steps, and the edges of the doorway were charred by the heat, some points even actively flaming.

Bolan nodded in satisfaction and then inched back until he was positioned just to the right of an open window. He detached an AN-M14 TH3 grenade from his LBE harness, primed it and lobbed it through the frame. A moment later the hand bomb exploded, scattering the interior with enough white phosphorous to ignite the combustibles of a small room.

Bolan delivered an M-26 fragmentation grenade behind that and moved toward the rear of the house well before it blew. Red-orange flames belched from the open window, but Bolan had already rounded the corner.

A trio of hardcases bailed from the interior of the house by way of a back door and right into Bolan's fire zone. He triggered a short blast that lifted the first target off his feet and dumped him in a heap on the mossy jungle floor. The second gunner turned in Bolan's direction with a look of complete shock on his face, only to take a full salvo of 5.56 mm hornets in the chest. The slugs ripped through lungs and heart as a torrent of blood exploded from his mouth. The third man barely had time to bring his weapon up before Bolan cut him down with a volley to the pelvis and abdomen. He dropped to his knees, triggering his weapon harmlessly into the loam as he toppled onto the ground face-first.

Bolan vaulted the steps as he pulled another thermate grenade from his LBE harness. He put his back to the wall, nudged the door open with his foot and gently lobbed the armed grenade inside. It exploded a moment later and brought with it two distinct screams of anguish. The Executioner waited a full ten seconds before carefully inching inside. The doorway opened onto a small hall that widened into a circular interior room. Patches of flame were everywhere, and Bolan stepped wisely to avoid any pools of phosphorous—they would surely burn straight through his boots and put a quick end to the show.

He advanced beyond the pair of motionless bodies with clothes and hair awash in flames and headed deeper into the bowels of the massive house. Only silence greeted him, but Bolan wasn't buying it. Cristobal was close—he could feel it. The crime lord's time had run out and he had an appointment with the Executioner, an appointment that could only result in one possible outcome. Death had just darkened his doorway.

And the reaper of that harvest had come in the form of a man called Bolan.

19

Paz eased off the trigger of his L86A1 machine gun and observed the pandemonium and destruction before him.

The myriad fires burning throughout the encampment cast shadows of dead or dying men against what remained standing of walls and trees. The movements coupled with the screams of the injured produced an eerie effect, like those derived from watching a horror B-movie. As Paz surveyed the scene, it solidified his agreement with Quinones's comments regarding Colonel Stone's reputation. The guy was a pure hell-raiser who had one hell of a way to get his message across.

The fact that they were close to securing a victory didn't concern him nearly as much as making sure Cristobal didn't escape. He'd been only partially truthful with Stone, but he made no apologies for it. Paz *did* want revenge for the indignities he'd suffered, sure, but even more he wanted to exact retribution for the way Cristobal had outwitted him in using Mariana as a spy. After the revelation and the subsequent escape, the BATF agent realized how much he'd really come to care for the woman. To find out she'd been playing him all the time was more than a betrayal. Now he hated her with every fiber of his being, and he intended to make sure neither she nor her master got away with it.

Even as Stone began his internal sweep, Paz withdrew from his firing position and gathered his weapon. He trotted the twenty some odd yards to where Quinones still lay in a patch of elephant grass that had grown in an area devoid of overhead foliage. The DEA man whipped out a pistol and nearly shot Paz.

"Shit," he snarled, still in a whisper, "don't ever frigging sneak up on me like that, dude."

"You okay?"

Quinones nodded slowly as he holstered his pistol. "Not a scratch. You?"

"I'm fine. Listen, I'm going in there to help Stone. If he gets back before I do, tell him I went looking for Cristobal."

"Damn it, Ignacio, he told us to wait here. You change the plan and go in there now, the guy's likely to mistake you for one of them and shoot your balls off."

Paz grimaced, acknowledging the possibility that Quinones was right but intent on setting things straight. "I don't care. I want that son of a bitch."

Quinones looked torn. "So all that crap back there about not wanting revenge was just blowing smoke."

"I didn't ask for this, and I sure as hell don't have to justify it to you, Quinones."

"No? Okay, maybe not, but what about Stone, huh? The guy risked his life to come down here and save your ass. You don't think you owe him something for that?"

"I wouldn't expect you to understand."

Quinones sighed. "Well…damn. If nothing else, I can't let you go it alone."

Paz considered that for a moment. Colonel Stone would already be livid when he found out Paz had disobeyed orders, but he'd be more incensed if he knew he dragged Quinones along. Still, it was a stupid man who tried to go it alone when someone offered help, and this guy seemed pretty good in a fight. At least he'd have backup if Cristobal managed to get the upper hand on him.

"All right, but we do it my way."

"Like you were going to do it Stone's?" Quinones shot back as he climbed to his feet. He hefted the over-and-under combo to chest level and indicated his readiness with a nod.

Paz turned and the two men ventured from the relative safety of the perimeter and into the hell zone. Paz couldn't dispel the feeling of shame for lying to Colonel Stone, but he saw this was as much his fight as it was the military man's, and he was duty bound to do all he could to ensure Cristobal and Mariana didn't get away. Firmly resolved to take back his honor, Paz gripped his weapon tighter as he led his ally toward absolute victory.

BOLAN'S SEARCH of the house proper turned up nothing, and as he made his exit the warrior began to wonder if Cristobal had left shortly after learning of his prisoner's escape. Somehow, he didn't deem it probable. A guy like Cristobal might have hidden to save his own neck, but he wouldn't run. Bolan left the house and began to scour the grounds for any resistance or a clue as to Cristobal's whereabouts. He didn't encounter any more troops and what few he found still alive were either incapacitated to the point they posed no threat or were just plain near death.

Bolan began to widen his search and eventually detected an unnatural break in the perimeter. He ventured down a path that could only have been man-made, conscious that it had somewhat of a slope to it. Bolan slowed, trading out the FNC for his Desert Eagle. He ventured ten paces or so, stopped to listen, then went another ten. Somewhere ahead he could hear a noise, almost like a drone or chugging, and as he drew closer it became apparent.

The sound of a cranking engine!

The Executioner stepped up to a trot, and as he drew nearer

he confirmed his original suspicions. It was a car engine, no doubt, and it sounded big like that of a truck or SUV. Bolan lost his footing once and went down on one knee. He tried to see what he'd slipped on but couldn't tell in the dark. His eyes suddenly caught a familiar shape, and he looked to his right slightly and spotted the body. Bolan leaned closer and realized it was one of Cristobal's crew. As his eyes adjusted, the coppery smell hit his nostrils and he realized he'd slipped on a trail of blood streaming from the body. Maybe he'd been hit during the assault. Bolan got to his feet, turned and set off once more in the direction of the whining engine.

"WHAT ARE YOU DOING, you moron?" Cristobal demanded. "Get us out of here before those hitters show up! What the hell is wrong with you?"

"It's fucking flooded, goddammit!" Cristobal's driver said as he tried once more to get the Jeep's engine started.

"Don't get smart with me," Cristobal said icily. "And get this piece of shit started or I'll put a bullet in you my damn self!"

"You're not going anywhere, Serafin," a voice said.

Both men looked to their left in shock to find Paz and a man they didn't recognize standing there with automatic weapons pointed at them. Cristobal could tell by the look in Paz's eyes that the guy had murder on his mind. No way! That *pinche* didn't have the fucking balls to kill him in cold blood, and especially not in front of a witness who Cristobal merely assumed to be another cop, maybe from Paz's outfit, maybe not.

"Now get your hands up!" Paz demanded.

Both men raised their hands, and Paz gestured with the muzzle of his weapon to indicate they should climb out of the Jeep. Cristobal's eyes flicked ever so imperceptibly to their rear as he turned his head in mock compliance but neither of the men saw the look. A smile played across the gang lord's lips even as he heard the first shot ring out. The bullet struck Paz in the left flank, just behind the crease of the armpit where it met his back. The impact pitched him forward into a nearby support holding up the roof of the makeshift vehicle shelter, and he hit the ground.

The other man whirled and tried to bring his autorifle to bear, but he was a heartbeat too late. The second round hit him dead center in the chest and slammed him into the door of the Jeep. The weapon clattered from his fingers and he staggered forward, collapsing on his knees. It appeared the bullet hadn't killed him, however. Mariana realigned her sights to fire another round into his head.

She never got the shot off.

Mariana's own skull suddenly exploded at nearly the same moment as a thundering report boomed through the amphitheater-like canopy provided by the mass of overhead trees. Mariana's lithe body left the ground and collided with a tree before sliding to the jungle floor in a dead heap. Cristobal quickly picked up his gun from inside the Jeep and pointed it blindly into the jungle. A tall, shadowy form seemed to materialize from the darkness, bringing with it the stench of spent cordite. The gang lord couldn't make out any distinct features, but he was big and muscular, and there was no mistaking the huge silver pistol in his fist.

"End of the line, Cristobal," the man said in an icy voice.

Before Cristobal could get a shot off, he was no more.

WITH THE DRIVER BEGGING for his life, the Executioner knew he could expect no trouble from the guy. He yanked him one-handed from the Jeep and bound his hands behind him with a zip of thick, plastic riot cuffs from the cargo pocket of his fatigues.

Bolan then turned his attention to Quinones, who had

finally managed to unfold himself from his position on the ground. He was breathing heavily and complaining about the severe pain in his chest, but other than that he appeared no worse for the wear.

The same could not be said for Ignacio Paz. The man lay on his back and blood seeped from his wound. Bolan had issued both of the men bulletproof vests. Quinones's had protected him quite effectively, but the woman's bullet had managed to strike at just the wrong point on Paz and passed straight through a vital organ. Bolan knew the round had hit the BATF agent's heart and possibly even a lung as there were pink, frothy bubbles at the corner of his mouth that increased with every expiratory wheeze.

"S-s-sorry, Colonel," Paz finally managed.

"Just hang tough, soldier," Bolan said. "We're going to get you help."

"Too…too late."

Bolan swallowed hard, knowing there wasn't a thing he could do. Any attempt to stop the bleeding or render aid would have been futile. He'd seen enough death to know when it loomed large, and he felt it squeeze his heart in the form of a throaty lump as he watched another good man sink into the depths of eternal rest. Damn! Why hadn't the guy just done as he'd been told? Whether Bolan had wanted to or not, he couldn't help but feel responsible for this poor soul. The guy had gone out for revenge, and it ultimately ended up killing him.

Still, the Executioner didn't judge Paz. This was a good man who lay dying before him. An honorable man.

"He-here's some…something I need you to do," Paz said as he reached to his fatigue pocket and withdrew a crumpled sheet of paper inside a crumpled plastic bag. He pressed it into Bolan's hand.

The Executioner felt the grip loosen before he pulled the bag

away and set Paz's arm gently on his stomach. Bolan looked
around, located a tarp in the back of the Jeep and unfolded it
with a snap of his wrists to cover the body. He deserved to be
honored that way. Bolan knew at some point they would be per-
forming a similar act back in the States, only then it would be
an American flag draped over a wooden coffin.

"He gone?" Quinones asked.

"Yeah," Bolan replied.

"I'm sorry, Colonel," the DEA agent said quietly. "I tried
to talk him out of it, but he just wouldn't hear it."

"Sometimes we do what we think we have to, Quinones,
even when others tell us it isn't right. Ignacio Paz died fighting
for what he believed in."

"You're saying there's honor in that?"

Bolan looked the man in the eyes and squeezed his
shoulder reassuringly. "Always."

Quinones looked down to see Bolan holding out the plastic
bag for him to take. "Oh, he left that with you, sir. I think he
wanted *you* to make sure it got to whoever he intended it for.
Probably his wife and kids."

"Maybe," Bolan said. "But I think it would be better if they
received it from one of his own. A brother cop."

Quinones looked at the plastic bag, nodded once and then
slowly took it from Bolan's grasp.

Epilogue

Stony Man Farm, Virginia

"Reports are still coming in, Striker, but things are looking up," Brognola announced.

"And with Serafin Cristobal out of the picture," Price added, "the MS-13's infrastructure is crumbling. Nearly every shot-caller in the organization is vying to take his place, and the infighting has considerably weakened their network."

"So much for solidarity in the ranks," Bolan replied.

"We also identified your mystery man," Price said, passing a folder to Bolan. "Within the MS-13 hierarchy he was known as Segador, a Spanish name that translates as 'reaper.' His real name was Andries Blood, originating from the Netherlands. Apparently he had gotten disqualified from almost every military academy and armed forces unit in northern Europe, so he took up training as a gun-for-hire and illegally entered the U.S. under an assumed identity."

"Do we know if he did Guerra?"

Brognola shrugged. "There's no way we can prove it, but we're pretty confident he did. The man you took prisoner down in El Salvador flipped on his late boss for a deal. He's providing the AG with plenty of insight into MS-13 operations."

"To say nothing of his implication of a dozen shot-callers throughout the U.S.," Price interjected. "I don't imagine it will be long before most of them are indicted, which should negate even a larger part of their operations."

"Yes," Brognola said. "It will be a very long time before they recover."

"If ever," Bolan agreed.

"Striker, the Man asked me to pass on a personal thanks to you. Your efforts have actually helped to strengthen political relations with the Salvadoran government. They have even agreed to step up their efforts in cooperating with the DEA to stem the drug trade, and other nations are starting to follow their example."

Price winked. "Didn't know your efforts would have such wide-reaching effects."

The warrior grinned. "All for one and one for all."

"Oh, yes," Brognola said, "that reminds me. Agent Quinones made a big stink about you."

"Oh?"

"Yes." Brognola chuckled. "It seems he's crediting you with single-handedly taking down Cristobal's little empire down there. Even insisted on putting you in for the Law Enforcement Medal of Valor."

"Save it for Ignacio Paz. He's the real hero." Bolan glanced at the wall clock and then pushed his chair from the table and rose.

Brognola looked up at his friend with raised eyebrows. "Going somewhere?"

The Executioner nodded. "I've been thinking about taking some R&R. Now seems as good a time as any."

"Any particular place in mind?" Price inquired.

"Sure, but I can't tell you, ma'am."

"Why not?"

"It's classified."

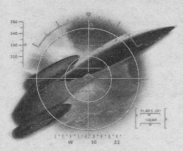

AleX Archer
SACRED GROUND

The frozen north preserves a terrible curse...

For the Araktak Inuits, the harsh subzero tundra is their heritage. Now a mining company has purchased the land, which includes the sacred Araktak burial site. Contracted by the mining company, archaeologist Annja Creed is to oversee the relocation of the burial site—but the sacred ground harbors a terrible secret....

Available March 2010 wherever books are sold.

www.readgoldeagle.blogspot.com

GRA23